They Call Me Junior

A Gay Love Story

By

Sheena Perry

Copyright

They Call Me Junior

Published by Sheena Perry Publishing

Edited by Sheena Perry

ISBN-10: 1-7321180-3-5
ISBN-13: 978-1-7321180-3-4

This is a work of fiction. Any references or similarities to actual events, real people, living or dead, or to the real locals intended to give the novel a sense of reality. Any similarity in other names, characters, places, and incidents are entirely coincidental.

The *Tea* on the Author

Sheena Perry is originally from Dallas, TX. She was raised by her teenage single mother, Tonya. Sheena is the oldest of two children. Sheena's mother fell prey to the booming crack cocaine era of the 1980's. Entrusting a close relative with the task of babysitting her two kids, Tonya left for work one day not realizing that the family member would leave them alone and call DCFS.

At tender age of three, Sheena and her brother were removed from the home and placed into separate foster homes. While her brother was placed into a fairly nice foster home, she however suffered unimaginable abuse at the hands of her foster parents. She went days without eating, was fed dog food and she was tied to a chair throughout the day. Her thighs are still branded with the markings from the tight ropes.

Her mother was able to quickly regain custody of both children. However, later the same year she was molested by her mother's fiancé. Immediately reporting the abuse to her mother, the monster was quickly apprehended and served a lengthy stint in prison. Prison did not stop Sheena's molester from issuing out death threats.

He was heavily involved in the drug world and his threats were taken very seriously. Sheena's mom relocated her small family to Columbus, GA. After experiencing such traumatic events, she became extremely shy and withdrawn. She was even mute for two years. The once bubbly outgoing little girl had been replaced by an insecure, self-loathing shell of her former self.

As she became older, Sheena would contemplate suicide numerous times to cope with the unfortunate cards she had been dealt. She had even developed an eating disorder in her mid-teens. Sheena's mother continued to battle with her drug addiction throughout her childhood and into her young adulthood. Sheena has always had a deep passion for reading and writing. Reading has always been her outlet to escape the obstacles that she faced on a daily basis.

She enjoys romance, mystery, horror, autobiographies, thrillers and urban novels. From an early age, Sheena had tutored kids much older than herself. Sheena particularly enjoys writing short stories and poetry. She currently lives in Florissant, MO. Despite her rough beginnings, she was able to conquer all of her hurdles and meet many of her goals.

She was able to purchase her first house at the age of 20. A year later she gave birth to her daughter, Aaliyah. Somehow, she managed to overcome the murder of her daughter's father, who was killed by the police when their daughter was just 4 months old. She is a Registered Nurse. Sheena has a master's degree in Nursing Education. She is currently in school pursing her Doctorate degree.

She works as a nursing professor at a major university and is the Director of Nursing at a long-term care facility. Sheena is also a licensed foster parent. Having had such a horrific experience during her time in foster care, she wanted to offer a safe home to children in need.

Please stay tuned for ***Inevitable Deceptions: The Heart's Journey to Nowhere 3*** which is Sheena's third and final installment of the series. She also co-wrote the children's book ***I Made You From Scratch: You Are Perfect*** with her daughter.

In addition to Inevitable Deceptions: ***The Heart's Journey to Nowhere 3***, she is currently working on two other books: ***Do No Harm: License to Kill and Taste Of Evil: A Collection Of 10 Unsettling Tales.*** She has also published novels such as ***The Girl Behind The Smile*** by Dornisha Goodrich, ***God Showed Me More***

Than Heaven by K.S. Fisher and ***The Living*** by Frank Washington. Please stay tuned!

I attribute my success to this – I never gave or took any excuse. – Florence Nightingale

Connect with Sheena

Visit her website at www.sheenaperrypublishing.com

Friend her on Facebook at www.facebook.com/sheena.p.rn

Link with her on LinkedIn at www.linkedin.com/in/sheena-perry-msn-rn-cne-22352486

Follow her on Twitter at www.twitter.com/sheenamperry

Follow her on Instagram at www.instagram.com/sheenamperry

You can also visit her business page at https://m.facebook.com/SheenaPerryPublishing/

Submissions for all genres are now open. Please submit the first 3-4 chapters of your manuscript for publishing consideration. Allow up to 30 days for a response. Complete contact information including name, address, contact number and email. Use 12 pt. font, double-spaced in manuscript style format. Email manuscripts to submissions@sheenaperrypublishing.com.

We look forward to hearing from you!

Dedication

I'd like to dedicate this book to all of those who have been on the receiving end of abuse. Always know that it is never your fault. You are not alone. Don't be ashamed. Be your own advocate; seek help immediately before it is too late. Do not let your abuser have power over you. Remember that if they've abused you once, chances are that they will strike again.

In loving memory of Michael Calvin Perry, Doris Marie Green, Carolyn Marie White, James Green, Samuel Keita DeBoise, Erin LeighAnna Nabe, Lennette Berry, Michael Perry, Jr, Paul Anthony Sheets, Sr and Pauline Roberts-Perry.

I love and miss you all more than anyone will ever know. Rest in paradise.

~Sheena

Table of Contents

The *Tea* on the Author

Connect with Sheena

Dedication

Acknowledgements

Chapter 1: “No Sob Stories”

Chapter 2: “Nobody’s Nigga”

Chapter 3: “Testing My Gangsta”

Chapter 4: “Netflix And Chill”

Chapter 5: “Indian Giver”

Chapter 6: “Daddy’s Girl”

Chapter 7: “Cat And Mouse”

Chapter 8: “Where I Wanna Be”

Chapter 9: “Family Man”

Chapter 10: “Cat Fished”

Chapter 11: “Article 134”

Chapter 12: “Meelah”

Chapter 13: “Blackmail”

Chapter 14: “Homo-Hetero”

Chapter 15: “Calm Before The Storm”

Chapter 16: “The Aftermath”

Chapter 17: “Dear Junior”

Chapter 18: “Overrated”

Chapter 19: "Black And Blue"

Chapter 20: "C.N.A."

Chapter 21: "Sweet Cheeks"

Chapter 22: "Shitfaced"

Chapter 23: "Living My Best Life"

Chapter 24: "Elastic Heart"

Chapter 25: "Don't Mess With Texas"

Chapter 26: "To Prep Or Not To Prep"

Chapter 27: "Branded"

Chapter 28: "Second Chances"

Chapter 29: "Blast From The Past"

Chapter 30: "From Darkness To Light"

Acknowledgements

To my loving mother, Tonya Perry, I appreciate you for always being my biggest cheerleader. You have always inspired me to challenge myself. You are the strongest person that I know. I love you so much Ma!

To my brother, Rico, we may not always see eye to eye but know that I will always love you to the moon and back. No one can make me laugh the way that you do. You are my best friend.

To my beautiful daughter, Aaliyah, the day that I had you was by far the happiest day of my life. You made me grow up overnight. You are growing into the most amazing young woman that I could ever ask for. I know that your dad is smiling down at you from heaven. I hope that I have always been a positive role model for you and that you realize that you are my biggest motivator. All of my accomplishments were achieved with you in mind. Remember the sky is the limit and that the word *never* is not a part of our vocabulary. I love you baby girl.

To my friends and colleagues that have put up with my endless brainstorms and offered words of encouragement, I thank you for everything. I'd also like to thank my test readers who have given me constructive criticism.

I'd also like to give a special thanks to my readers who have purchased, downloaded and rated my books. You will never know how much your love and support means to me.

Lastly, I'd like to thank the good Lord above. Thank you for continuing to bless me. Without you, none of this would be possible.

~Sheena

*****WARNING*****

THIS NOVEL CONTAINS STRONG LANGUAGE, BROKEN ENGLISH, SEX, VIOLENCE, AND VULGAR SITUATIONS WHICH MAY BE OFFENSIVE TO SOME READERS.

« Chapter 1 No Sob Stories »

I DO NOT HAVE ANY traumatic childhood sob stories for you. Overall, I had an amazing childhood. I wasn't raised by a single mom in the projects. I wasn't emasculated. My siblings weren't fathered by different men. My parents were married and both gainfully employed. Neither of them drank excessively or was strung out on drugs. We all attended church every Sunday. I wasn't molested by a relative or a deacon. We vacationed more than most. I never experienced a hungry day. With all of that being said, I'm sure you are wondering what the hell I could possibly have to talk about.

What's a story without sexual abuse, drug addicted parents and poverty? While I have lived what some would consider a charmed life, nothing is perfect. My parents doted on me, my sister and my brother. I was the oldest boy, so I proudly carried my father's name. My father was an officer in the military and had extremely high expectations of all of us. Sometimes it could be difficult living up to his expectations. He was a perfectionist and could be difficult to please most of the time. Mama was a school nurse. As a matter of fact, she was the school nurse at Dartmouth Academy where my siblings and I attended school.

My siblings were bothered and embarrassed sometimes by our mother working at our school, however I absolutely loved it. It was nice being able to see mama whenever I wanted to. Plus, every day during my lunch period I sat in her office and we ate our lunches together. My mama was very pretty. Her skin was a beautiful shade of russet. Her golden orbs appeared to dance in the sunlight. Her pouty lips and deep set dimples were features that we'd all inherited from her. Her naturally curly hair was always kept short and neat. It framed her oval shaped face perfectly. At five foot eleven, her lean curvy figure kept the male faculty finding reasons to visit the nurses' office throughout the day.

She was so in love with my father that I don't think she ever really took notice of how much they fawned over her. My dad was no slouch in the looks department either. His freckled skin was the color of butterscotch. His sandy brown hair was cut short in a flawless fade. His dark brown eyes were covered by mile long lashes that many women envied.

He typically sported a clean-shaven face, but my mama went wild when he rocked a little stubble from time to time. He always had a seriousness about him, but always had a soft spot for his family. He was six foot five inches and was ripped with muscles. My parents were an attractive pair who produced even more attractive offspring.

My name is Merlon P. Hilton, Jr, but everyone calls me Junior. My sister's name is Aimee Hilton. She is the oldest out of the three of us. My little brother's name is Jonah. While two years separated me and Aimee, I am only a year older than Jonah. Despite me being older than Jonah, he looked like the oldest between the two of us. I was very small for my age and what some would consider sickly. I was diagnosed with sickle cell anemia at age one. I was a frequent visitor of our nearby hospital throughout my childhood, but in some odd way it seemed to make us all that much closer. I was particularly close to mama and Aimee.

Aimee was my protector. I was what everyone considered soft and sensitive, but my sister was a fire cracker. She didn't play when it came to me and Jonah. Jonah closely resembled our father. He possessed his reddish hair and freckles. Aimee and I were mama's twins. We were dark and lovely, just like her. We had also inherited her golden colored eyes that Jonah often voiced he wished he had. Jonah was heavily into sports so he and my dad shared that common bond. I really wasn't into any sports to be perfectly honest. I often wondered if my dad was embarrassed by that fact. I bet he wished he had named Jonah after him instead of me. After all, Jonah resembled and behaved most like him.

We were a blessed military family. Unlike a lot of other families, we weren't forced to uproot our lives every few years. Apparently, the majority of the moving occurred prior to us being born. My dad joined the military and married mama when they were both just eighteen. They had been high school sweethearts and had beaten a lot of odds placed against them.

I enjoyed hearing about all of the wonderful places they had traveled to as a result of his military career. People were often fascinated when they learned that Jonah and I were born in Korea. We'd often tell people that we were Korean and they would always have the most confused expressions etched in their faces. His military benefits also enabled mama to obtain her nursing degree without having to go into debt. It was all paid for in full.

None of it happened overnight. After ten wonderful years of marriage, they finally decided to have Aimee. Me and Jonah soon followed. Shortly after Jonah was born, we relocated to the states. They had purchased a modest four-bedroom, three-bathroom home in Frisco, TX. We wanted for absolutely nothing. We had a slew of cousins in Dallas that we visited every chance we got. Daddy fired up the grill most weekends as we played with water balloons and super soakers to keep cool. Nothing compared to that scorching Texas heat.

I suppose in hindsight I had always been a little different. My favorite colors were pink and purple while most boys like Jonah loved blue. I loved tea time and playing with dolls with Aimee more than playing video games and basketball with Jonah. I think my parents overlooked a lot of small details because I was so sick all the time. I knew they just wanted me to be happy. Oftentimes, Aimee was the only one out of my two siblings willing to play with me, so it was only natural that I gravitated more towards the feminine laced games. I could play most of Aimee's games from the hospital bed.

I can recall one hurtful incident when I was about five years old. I remember it was a Saturday because my mom was away at a

Saturday clinical. Aimee and I were playing dress up. We had done each other's hair and makeup and we were looking quite fierce...if I must say so myself. I have always been what you might call androgynous. I was so pretty that most people assumed that I was a little girl.

My mom thought my long silky hair was so beautiful that she could never bring herself to cut it. My hair was nearly waist length by the time I reached five. My mom either put it in a ponytail or braided it for me. My dad being a military man hated seeing his oldest son running around with a ponytail, however, my mother wouldn't hear about cutting my hair.

I remember Aimee and I prancing around and dramatically cat walking down our make shift runway in mama's heels. We were giggling and having a good old time just being ourselves. I was so into my sexy strut that the stinging sensation to my backside caught me off guard. I watched as a look of horror crept over Aimee's delicate face as the realization of what was occurring came to me. Quickly spinning in my oversized heels, I was met with the furiously disgusted look of my dad. He had a belt in his hand and was preparing to swat at me again.

"Boy, what the hell do you have on?! If you do not take that damned sissy stuff off, I will hurt you! No son of mine is going to be a faggot." He yelled which scared the daylight out of me since it was rare that he ever yelled.

He was always so calm, cool and collected. He just simply gave us "the look" and we stopped in our tracks.

I didn't understand what the words sissy or faggot meant, although, I had been called those words before at school. I recall crying hysterically and pleading with my dad to stop hitting me with the belt.

"Daddy, I'm sorry for being a sissy! I'll stop being a faggot! I won't do it anymore! Please daddy. I'm sorry!" With that I cowered into the fetal position and waited for my dad to grow tired of hitting me.

I could hear Aimee crying too somewhere in the background. She always hurt when I hurt. Four-year-old Jonah could also be heard somewhere in the distance, however, instead of crying...he was laughing uncontrollably. Sometimes I really hated him. He could be so evil.

After some time, my dad picked me up and took me into the bathroom. Placing me on my feet in front of the mirror he ordered me to wipe my makeup off. The entire time I scrubbed my face, I watched my dad who was standing behind me. He looked so hurt, disgusted and disappointed. After wiping the makeup off as best I could, daddy grabbed and then unraveled the bun that Aimee had placed on top of my head. My long mane was flowing beautifully down my back. Ignoring my physical pain, I couldn't help but to notice how gorgeous I was.

Distracting me from my conceited thoughts, my dad barked, "I don't give a damn about what Melanie says. You're getting a haircut today! She's going to be furious, but she will get over it!" He spoke more so to himself than to me.

After he retrieved a pair of scissors, I attempted to run, but he quickly caught me by my damn hair and threatened to whoop me again if I made any other attempts to run.

With every clipping sound the scissors made, I wailed like I had lost my best friend. I couldn't believe that he was cutting my beautiful hair. How was I going to look afterwards? After a while, my vision was completely blurred by tears, so I didn't know what I looked like anymore. After some time lapsed, I heard him set the scissors down and then the loud buzzing of the clippers took over the bathroom. I just stood there sobbing with my eyes closed. It felt like we were in there for hours as my dad expertly cut my hair.

At some point I heard him say, "Now that's more like it. Now you look like my son. Go on and take a bath and then take your narrow butt to bed. Don't let me catch you in makeup and heels anymore Junior."

"Yes sir," was all I said as I prepared to follow his orders.

When mama arrived home around seven-thirty in the evening, all hell broke loose when she noticed my newly acquired fade. She let our dad have it! She refused to sleep in their marital bed for a while after that incident. Call it paranoia, but I never really felt that my dad looked at me the same after that day. I don't think that I ever looked at him the same either. I always felt a strong need to please him, however, I never felt that my best was ever good enough. Why did I have to be different?

« Chapter 2 Nobody's Nigga »

DARTMOUTH ACADEMY WENT all the way to the eighth grade. I think it was around the sixth grade that I started to have little crushes. I realized very early on that I was particularly fond of one of my male classmates named Corey. There were several girls in my class that I identified as being pretty, but I just did not see them the same as I did Corey. They didn't give me butterflies in my tummy the way he did. It was in the sixth grade, however, that I began to surround myself around the girls. With my pretty boy looks, my reputation as the ladies' man began.

Corey was into all the sports and also ran track. So I called myself joining the track and basketball teams in order to be in his presence. Of course, I had to take extra precautions and stay hydrated in order to avoid exacerbating my sickle cell anemia. I turned out to be an extremely fast runner, however, I was a mediocre ball player at best. I think my dad was finally proud of me for the first time in my life when I decided to play sports. My entire family made it to every race and game that I had. Even Jonah began to look up to me for the first time. This motivated me to go harder.

While Corey was one of the most beautiful people that I had ever laid my honey colored orbs on, he was a little on the homely side. He didn't wear the latest pair of sneakers, nor did he ever sport any overpriced designer clothes. Our school mandated that the students wore uniforms, and many of us absolutely hated it. I could tell that Corey only had two sets of uniforms based on the holes in them and by the permanent stains on them.

They were also a little on the tight side. His uniform pants were definitely classified under the high-water category. My boy was walking around with Steve Urkel's on. He was much too precious to be strutting around in those rags. Despite his tattered clothing, he was as confident as could be. If he was embarrassed or self-conscious, it surely didn't show. He was quiet and typically kept to himself. During the rare moments when I was blessed to see him smile, my heart melted.

Although we were just in the sixth grade, Corey was quickly approaching six feet. He had to be at least five foot ten. His slender frame was topped with muscles that resulted from his athleticism. His light brown skin beautifully framed his body. His thick eye brows and long lashes overshadowed his dark intense eyes. He had the thickest, pinkest lips and I knew those bad boys were soft as silk. He wore his hair in a low fro that could use a fresh line up. Perhaps Corey's sexiest feature was the gap between his two front teeth. That shit drove me nuts! Literally!

Despite excelling and being number one on all of our school's sports teams, he didn't hang with any of the cliques. He was a loner and that fascinated me because I was too up until the girls started swarming around me that year. I didn't have any guy friends, but I was hopeful that he would be.

One day while eating lunch with my mom, the perfect opportunity came when she handed me a bag filled with new uniforms, socks and underwear. She then asked, "Junior, aren't you in class with Corey Wilkerson?"

"Yes ma'am. We play ball and run track together too." I curiously gushed.

"Well I need you to give him this bag of clothes. Oh, here are some toiletries too. I'm sick of that baby running around here looking like no one loves him. He comes to my office hungry nearly every morning. I don't know what his parents are up to, but he deserves better. Now that school is already in session, Walmart has a great sale on uniforms, so I picked him up a few items. He is a little taller than Jonah, so these should fit just fine. Make sure he gets these please, son."

"Yes mama. I will give them to him." I beamed finishing up my turkey sandwich. I finally had a reason to talk to him.

Later that day in the locker room, I spotted Corey in a corner changing into a uniform. Tears stung at the corners of my eyes when I noticed bruises varying in colors and sizes all over his torso. The large holes in his underwear didn't evade me either. What the hell was his story? What was wrong with his parents? It took everything in me to refrain from taking my boo into my arms and telling him everything would be alright from that point on.

Lost in my captain save a hoe thoughts, I was completely oblivious to the fact that Corey had finished dressing and was now peering down at me with a pissed expression etched into his handsome face. Once I realized that he was no longer across the room, but was now hoovering over my slight frame, I gulped hard and stammered, "Wha...what did you ssssayyyyy?"

"I asked your sissy ass what you were staring at nigga?!" He repeated loudly.

I glanced around and noticed that luckily everyone else had already left the locker room. Although I didn't quite feel courageous, I refused to be bullied by anyone.

"I'm not a sissy, nor am I a nigga. I wasn't staring at you, I was thinking about something that happened earlier. But since you're here, my mom is the school nurse here and asked me to give you these bags." I quickly offered, hoping to avoid an ass whooping.

His scowl appeared to soften a little as he blinked a few times. He then glanced at the bags in my outstretched arm before slowly reaching for it.

I smiled as he quickly sifted through them, eyeing their contents. He then looked back at me and growled, "Nigga, tell your mom thanks, but I'm not a fucking charity case." With that, he attempted to hand the bags back to me.

When I refused to take them back, he placed them on the ground. I felt my lips tighten as I grew pissed off with his ungrateful actions.

Refusing to take the bags back I stated, "Look, I've told you once and now I'm telling you again, I'm nobody's nigga. My mama told me to bring you those bags and that's what I'm doing. No offense, but I'm more afraid of a beat down from her than I am from you. Take it or leave it, the shit has been delivered." With that I angrily stormed off, however, I didn't go far.

Once I turned the corner of the locker room, I quietly peeked back around the corner to see what his next actions were going to be.

His back was facing me and I could see him staring down at the two bags. After what seemed like forever, he slowly bent down to retrieve those bags. A smile slowly crept over my face as I watched him place the bags into his locker.

« Chapter 3 Testing My Gangsta »

AFTER I DELIVERED those bags to Corey, he went back to ignoring me like he always had. It was a little difficult since mama had upgraded his uniforms, he was now sexier than ever. Hell, even the group of girls that I hung out with took notice. It wasn't easy pretending not to be upset and jealous by my friends lusting over my man. My friend Nu-Nu was even bold enough to slip him a note asking him to be her boyfriend. I could've choked her fat ass for pushing up on Corey.

Actually home girl wasn't fat in a literal sense. In fact, her body was on point! That overgrown heifer was shaped like a young Trina. How could my little scrawny ass compete with that? Plus, I was sure that I was far from his type. After all, I possessed a dick and a pair of balls just as he did. I often felt that I was probably the only kid in school with these sissy thoughts.

Of course, Corey took Nu-Nu's bait and agreed to be her boyfriend. Their union was bittersweet for obvious reasons. I hated them being together because I wanted him for myself. On the flip side, with them being together, he hung around our group more often. We even exchanged words occasionally. I always had to play it cool in his company. I acted tough and unaffected in his presence while on the inside I was squealing like a little bitch.

It took everything in me not to look at him for too long. I remembered what happened the last time I did. Instead, my glances were limited to fragmented ogling as I mentally stored images of him in my mind. He was so beautiful. Did I already say that? If I did, my bad. Why couldn't I have the same feelings of lust for the girls that I surrounded myself with?

At some point I also obtained my first girlfriend, Namiko. She was the most beautiful girl that I had ever laid eyes on. She was the perfect blend of her African American and Japanese heritage. Her beauty fascinated me almost as much as Corey's, however, as pretty as she was, I was not *sexually* attracted to her. I'm pretty sure my dad was more thrilled about me dating Namiko than I was. Namiko was a sweet girl, but to be perfectly honest, I needed her in order to mask my true dark desires.

I played my part as the dutiful boyfriend well. I held her books, opened doors, never forgot our anniversaries and was always the perfect gentleman. I simply mimicked how my father acted towards my mother. While our occasional kisses were sweet and soft, they did absolutely nothing for me. I only initiated them so that I could perfect my kissing technique for my man in the future.

Being with Namiko had its ups and downs much like any other relationship. My biggest challenge was constantly having to defend my position in her life. She was by far the prettiest girl in school and attracted a lot of admirers. She was the head cheerleader and was as smart as she was beautiful. I personally didn't care one way or the other if we were together, however, it was all about the damn principle. Those fools couldn't have her for the simple fact that they didn't approach me about the subject man to man. Instead they thought that they could muscle her away from me.

What they failed to realize was that although my feelings for Namiko were platonic, baby girl loved her some me! She was deeply in love with me and as loyal as they came. I never understood her deep attraction to me. Now don't get me wrong, I was a sexy beast myself, but she could've had any guy she wanted.

Why did she choose me? Even if I gave Namiko her walking papers, she still wouldn't be interested in any of them. Of course that never stopped them from testing my gangsta. I was small for my age and wasn't much of a fighter, but for some reason fools always wanted to jump me. They never approached me for a clean, fair fight.

One day as I was leaving the gym to get ready to go home, I was approached by Vasti, J-Boog and Lil Trey. They were brothers. In fact, J-Boog and Lil Trey were twins. Vasti was the leader of the pact and I knew that he was the one looking to win over Namiko's affections. Now let me paint you a picture of what Vasti looked like.

He was about five foot eight inches. Approximately one-hundred and sixty pounds. Not too bad, right? Well that fool looked like the rapper Chamillionaire in the face. I was convinced that he was half chimp and half human. Then he had the nerve to have sandy blonde hair! Let's move on, because I'm getting nauseous just thinking about his struggle faced ass!

Anyway, as soon as I spotted the three of their trouble making asses, I knew they meant me harm.

"What's up, fag? Didn't I tell your punk ass to break it off with Nami? She is too much woman for your bitch ass. Do you two go shopping together and share makeup tips? What does she see in your soft ass?" Vasti spat with disgust.

"Screw all three of you punks! I'm sick of y'alls jealous asses trying to fight me every day over *my girl.* You chimps...I mean chumps can jump me every day, but Nami will never like your ugly ape looking ass! If you are going to fight me then do less talking and get it over with. My girl is waiting for me to come over and tap that ass." I said gesturing towards my watch. I was lying of course. We had never knocked boots before.

This seemed to enrage Vasti as I noticed him toss his books down and charge in my direction.

Closing my eyes, I prepared to be struck by six fists. After several moments without feeling their highly anticipated knuckles, I slowly opened my eyes...one at a time. The sight before me came as a complete surprise. There Corey was standing in a boxer's stance ready to take on all three of my bullies. Seeing him, suddenly gave me a little courage. I couldn't leave my boo to fight my battle alone. All of a sudden, I leapt forward and wind-milled my way over to those bastards.

I heard, "What the fuck?!" Come from their direction as I felt strong hands pulling me back towards the opposite direction.

All I could think about was how amazing Corey smelled as J-Boog yelled, "Man fuck those sissies! We will catch Sweet Cheeks by himself sooner or later. Let's go to Rally's. Black is working today, so you know what that means!"

Turning to face Corey and making eye contact with him gave me butterflies. Damn that boy knew he was just too fine! He appeared to be inspecting my face for any signs of injuries. His expression then changed into one of annoyance.

"There you go with that staring shit man. What I tell you about that shit? Come on, I'll walk your nonfighting ass home." He offered.

I remained silent, but I twerked internally.

Once we reached my house, mama was checking our mailbox. Her face lit up when she noticed Corey with me.

"Hello boys! Corey, I hope you're staying for dinner. Come on in and get yourselves ready for supper." She instructed.

I was elated when he didn't object.

As we entered my house, I noticed as Corey's eyes examined one item then the next. My mom was a huge art fan and our house was peppered with some of the most beautiful paintings. While a lot of our furniture appeared to be top of the line, mama was certainly a great bargain hunter. We were far from rich, but my parents worked extremely hard to ensure that we were far from stressing about our next meal as well.

I decided to take Corey on a tour of our house, saving my bedroom for last. Once we reached my room, Corey proceeded to walk straight in and cop a squat on my Queen sized bed without an invitation. He better be lucky that I loved him, because I didn't allow just anybody to sit their funky ass on my bed.

Breaking me from my thoughts, he stated, "Man, you got a really nice crib. Ya parents must be ballin' fa real yo." He complimented…at least I thought so.

"Hey thanks, but no they aren't ballin', mama just knows how to shop. She always tells me that school nurses are probably the most underpaid nurses in the profession. My dad is in the military and has been for a while, so I guess he does okay." I offered.

"I think its dope how your parents are still together. I never even met my real father. Our house is nothing like this either. You are lucky." Corey lowly replied.

For the first time I realized that I knew nothing about him…or his family. Who was this beautiful Adonis? He was so mysterious to me.

"Sooooo…so…do you have any sisters or brothers? What does your mama do for a living? Where's your crib at?" I curiously stammered. I tried my damndest to mimic his use of slang. I only prayed that it sounded as cool to him as it did in my head.

He looked at me for a few moments as if he were putting a lot of thought into his answer.

He then replied, "I have an older sister, Adryenne. She received a full academic scholarship to Harvard. My mama sells her ass for a living and is rarely home, so I basically take care of myself. Her pimp stops by and kicks my ass whenever he is pissed at her or if she's gone MIA. We live in the projects off of Normandy. The only reason I was able to attend a school in this district is because coach took pity on me and allowed me to use his address. He used to come to the park in the projects and watch the kids play ball. I guess he saw my potential."

I was truly stunned by Corey's home life and his willingness to discuss the most intimate details of his life with me. I couldn't believe that he had to live through so much, yet he never missed a day of school or a game. I admired his strength. Hell, his place in my heart had just taken over my entire right ventricle. It wasn't until I felt a pillow hit the left side of my face that I realized someone had cut a few onions and I had tears streaming down my face.

"Nigga, whatchu crying for?! I'm going to be alright. I've been getting by for years and in the end…I'll have the final laugh. You just watch!" He vowed.

"What did I tell you about calling me that, man?!" I shouted as I wiped my face with my shirt.

Before he could respond, mama was calling us down to eat. Giving him the evil eye, I responded, "Come on, mama hates it when we are late."

Over dinner I could tell that everyone was trying to ignore the ravenous way in which Corey consumed his food. Mama was a great cook and all, but DAMN! My boo could eat!!! I couldn't help but to wonder when he had last eaten. He attended school so I was certain he had eaten there. So why was he so hungry now? I hadn't eaten since lunch, but I still ate like a civilized human being. What was really going on?!

I told my family about how I was nearly jumped by three guys until Corey saved me. Of course this revelation reserved a spot for Corey in the hearts of my family as well. They instantly took to him and he became like a third son to my parents. However, my feelings for him were anything but brotherly. As time went on he had practically moved in and my mom gave him a key of his own.

Corey had taken me to his house once to pick up a few things and after telling my parents about the condition of the small apartment, none of us wanted him going back. He only stopped by occasionally. Although my mom was a mandated reporter, she assured Corey that his secret was safe as long as he stayed with us. It was hard to believe that his mom didn't care about his whereabouts or well-being. I had yet to meet her. Corey never talked about her much, but he bragged about Adryenne a lot. I looked forward to meeting her one day. She was studying Law and seemed to be doing well in Boston.

My mom kept up with clothing and feeding Corey as if he were her own child. They couldn't call him dusty anymore. My baby had glowed up! The bullies left me alone once they saw that he and I had become close. Attending the same school, participating in the same sports and living in the same house...sharing a room was like a dream come true. When we weren't studying, playing sports or listening to music, we double dated.

It was still difficult for me. As I made out with Namiko, all I could think about was Corey and how I'd rather be swapping spit with *him*. It always broke my heart to see him and his girlfriend together. He always seemed so attentive and into her. Why didn't he look at me like that?

« Chapter 4 Netflix And Chill »

IT WASN'T UNTIL THE eighth grade that I finally lost my virginity to Corey. Well…not exactly to Corey, but in a way I did. We had both been dating our girlfriends for a while and the pressures to have sex were at an all-time high. Personally, I was indifferent on the matter. I was only interested in busting it wide open for one real guy…yet he wasn't an option.

I remember Me, Corey, Namiko and Nu-Nu all going over to Nu-Nu's house to 'Netflix and chill'. Her mom was working late and her dad was away on a business trip. Her house was nice and well-kept. She was an only child, so her parents spoiled her rotten. The girls cooked us some cheeseburgers and fries while I whooped Corey's ass at Call of Duty on Nu-Nu's PS2. He always claimed that I cheated, since I never lost a game. What he failed to realize was during my long stints in the hospital, sometimes all I had were my video games to keep me company. The fact was, no one could beat me at any video game.

After growing tired of beating Corey, we decided to eat. The food was great. We scarfed our food down in record time and decided to go listen to music in Nu-Nu's bedroom. Her room was the typical pink, purple and white princess style room. It was time for her parents to give her room a more mature look. Hell, their little princess was now fucking.

After joking around and shooting the breeze for a while, I noticed that Corey and Nu-Nu had begun to get a little frisky with one another. They had been having sex for some time now, but I had never witnessed them going at it. As hard as I wanted to not look, I couldn't help but to look on with envy as I watched my man and his girlfriend strip down to their birthday suits in front of me and Namiko.

She looked shocked too at first but, then a look of pure arousal took over her pretty face. Her already chinky eyes didn't even appear to be open anymore as I felt her taking my swollen member into her tiny hand. She caught me completely off guard. I tore my attention away from my man and glanced down at my girlfriend's hand and then into her eyes. Lust was written all over her face. She wanted to fuck me. And I wanted to fuck *him*. She and I had fooled around dozens of times, but we never went all the way. I could never acquire and maintain an erection.

Today was a different day. It was now or never. I slowly removed both of our clothes. Luckily, Namiko's eyes were closed because I could not keep my eyes off of Corey's beautifully sculpted ass, as his cheeks clenched and relaxed with each thrust, he made into Nu-Nu. I was so horny that precum began to drip from the tip of my uncut member. Namiko and I were lying horizontally at the foot of the full-sized bed, so I was able to get the perfect view of Corey's balls banging against Nu-Nu's asshole.

Redirecting my attention back to Nami, I applied a condom to my six inch stick. I then kissed her as I began to finger her slippery pussy. While she didn't stink, I always found the natural scent of pussy to be a huge turn off. I didn't like it and couldn't get past it. Honestly, my dick started to soften, until I glanced back up at Corey. I kept my eyes there as I placed the tip of my dick at Nami's entrance. As I pushed forward, both Nami and I drew in sharp breaths. Her pussy did feel great actually. She just wasn't what or who I wanted. As I stroked in and out of her, she lightly scratched my back.

As badly as I wanted to focus on what Corey was doing, I had to ensure that I was being gentle with Nami. It was her first-time having sex too, and I needed to disengage the selfish side of me that only wanted to fulfill my desires. Naturally, since it was my first time too, I seriously wanted to jackhammer her, but I composed my selfishness and delivered long slow strokes to her tight canal for a whopping four minutes.

The excitement and the pleasure were just too much for me to handle. If Nami was disappointed in my rapid performance, she never mentioned it to me. I made a silent promise to myself that I'd put forth more of an effort the next time we made love. I just prayed that my little soldier would be able to stand to attention without Corey's presence. Just as that thought came about, I watched in awe as his ass muscles flexed and his balls appeared to be having spasms.

My baby roared as he delivered stiffened strokes to Nu-Nu as he unloaded into her unprotected womb. That was perhaps the most hurtful, yet sexiest sight I had ever seen. That nut should've been planted inside of me.

« Chapter 5 Indian Giver »

BY THE TIME I reached high school, I had given up on basketball. I wasn't all that great at it anyway, plus I was much smaller than the other players. I was a beast on the track though. I almost always won first place and the room that I still shared with Corey was filled with numerous ribbons and trophies that he and I had accumulated together over the years.

I was facing some of my loneliest times during that period. I prayed for God to make me normal. I wanted to lust over girls and be happy with Namiko, but something was always missing. I was tired of pretending with her. I had to pretend to be jealous. I had to feign being angry after our stupid arguments. I even had to fake being turned on and most of my orgasms. My acting skills were certainly Oscar worthy. The truth was, I cared about my girlfriend, but I wanted nothing more than friendship.

I found myself picking fights with her just so that I could give her the silent treatment for a week or so. She was a great girl and certainly deserved to be treated better than I treated her. I never understood what made her stand by me when she could've easily gotten with someone who would have died to be on the receiving end of her affections. Unfortunately, her love for me was unwavering and I never seemed to be able to shake her.

During the times when she cried and questioned why I didn't want to be with her, I wanted to come clean and tell her the truth so badly. I wanted to assure her that it was nothing that she did or didn't do. It was me…all me. I could never bring myself to tell the girl that I was supposed to love that my heart would never belong to her no matter what she did. I hated wasting her time, but she was convinced that we were soulmates.

So instead of breaking her heart, I continued stringing her along. For me, it was easier. I didn't want the confrontation that I was sure would follow. My family loved her and had already discussed how adorable our Blasian babies would be. They definitely didn't make things any easier for me.

My little brother was trailing in me and Corey's footsteps and was beginning to make a name for himself at school. He had always told anyone who would listen that he was going to make it to the pros and with his talents and confidence none of us doubted him. Jonah vowed that if he didn't make it into the NBA then he would join the military like my father. Our father was his everything.

I on the other hand didn't have the slightest clue as to what I wanted to do after graduation. I loved helping people and could see a future in the healthcare field, however, I knew that my macho father wasn't going for that. No son of his was going to do any "sissy" work.

My health had always posed an issue for me. Statistically speaking, I often wondered if I would live to reach an old age. I knew that sickle cell anemia tended to reduce the average sufferer's life expectancy drastically. I nearly lost my battle during the summer proceeding my sophomore year. I was sicker than I had ever been during my prior episodes. I was in excruciating pain and truly felt that the end was near for me. I had truly given up and was tired of battling myself from within.

My family visited me regularly and prayed over me nonstop. I had no appetite and was forced to have a nasogastric tube placed. I couldn't stomach the Ensure supplements they tried to encourage me to drink. My days were spent feeling sorry for myself and browsing my social media timelines. Everyone else's lives appeared to be so uncomplicated.

I know we should never question God or the plans he's

already outlined for each of us, however, it was difficult to keep my faith when he allowed me to experience such misery. I didn't deserve it. After being hooked up to oxygen, IV fluids and a PCA pump for a little over a month, I was eventually discharged home. I was ordered to remain on bedrest and to take it easy.

During my near death experience, I realized just how short life was. It made me realize that I could no longer live a lie. I refused to jeopardize my happiness for the sake of appeasing others. I finally mustered up the strength to break things off with Nami. It hurt me to have to hurt her, but I had to let her go because I loved her too much to continue wasting her time and taking her love for me for granted.

Of course, she took it hard and dogged me out on the same social media sites that kept me preoccupied during my convalescence. It was okay though. I felt as if a huge burden had been lifted and I could now divert my full attention to the things that were truly important.

To my delight, Corey was by my side through it all. He spent every moment possible helping me during my recovery. One evening while my parents were out having their weekly date night, Corey and I had crept in the liquor cabinet. We were drunk as hell and debating who the five top rappers of all time were.

"Nigga, you hardly ever listen to rap, so your judgment is way off! Did you really say Will Smith?! You are buggin' for real yo! I tell you what though, a nigga is horny as fuck, but my shorty is on her period. Man, mother nature is the original cockblocker! I'm not ready to get my red wings just yet. Why do these broads have to bleed so damn much?! Uhhhhh!!!" Corey drunkenly exclaimed.

I cracked up laughing at his silly ass.

"I have a solution to your problem, but you have to be open minded." I suggested.

"Nigga, what is your solution to relieving this twelve-inch woody?"

"First of all, stop calling me that. Secondly, promise you won't get mad..."

"Muthafucka, if yo ass don't get to the fucking point..."

"Alright, alright. You're an angry drunk. What I was about to say before I was rudely interrupted is that we can get each other off. I mean, if you want to. I'm horny too. I figure since we are both horny and there isn't any pussy around that we could pleasure one another." I boldly stated hoping he wouldn't whoop my already weakened ass.

He was silent for a few moments and I could tell his mind was going a mile a minute.

"Yo Junior man, I'm not a faggot. I love women. I love pussy...not dick. So lay your ass down and sleep off the alcohol."

"Corey, what are you afraid of? I see the way that you look at me and you already know I'm feeling you. You can't be that blind. I'm not trying to label or categorize you, but you have to feel the chemistry between us." That alcohol had me feeling myself and going for the gusto. I was fearless.

"Muthafucka, I was raised by a fucking crackhead! I ain't scared of shit!!!"

"Then what are you waiting for?" I challenged.

With that Corey roughly pressed his lips up against mine. Fireworks were coursing through my veins. I hungrily devoured his lips as involuntary moans escaped from mine. I couldn't believe that this was finally happening. He broke our kiss and ordered me to remove my clothes. I did as I was told and watched him as he did the same. He was so sexy to me. His eyes never left mine as we disrobed.

I felt ashamed once I compared his dick size to mine. His pipe was nearly twice as large as mine in both length and girth. My thoughts were quickly removed from the forefront of my mind once he kneeled down in front of me and took my meager member into his warm mouth. I nearly fainted from the amazing feelings that he was giving me. Namiko and I had never given one another oral sex, so this was all very new to me.

Corey was so skilled that I couldn't help but to wonder if he had done it before. As my hips begin to thrust in and out of his face, the doorbell caused us both to jump up and hurriedly redress ourselves. I then bolted for the door to see who dared to interrupt the moment I had been dreaming of for years.

Peering through the peephole, I saw an unfamiliar woman standing there. I swiftly opened the door with a sour look on my face.

"Hello, is Corey here?" The woman asked.

Although she looked as if she had lived a rough life, she was still very pretty. The resemblance was uncanny.

"May I ask what this is regarding?" I asked the woman.

The woman sucked what teeth she had remaining and hissed, "I was told that Corey has been staying here. He is my son and I want him back!!!"

« Chapter 6 Daddy's Girl »

I SOFTLY WEPT INTO my pillow as the Vocal Bible's, Full Moon album serenaded in the background. Brandy knew she had some pipes on her! When Corey's mother came to pick him up, I felt as if my heart had been snatched from my body. To make matters worse, she had withdrawn him from our school and I had lost all contact with him.

Apparently, Corey's mother had gotten herself cleaned up and there wasn't anything that my parents could do. She was now sober, had moved into a house and was trying to do right by him now. What I couldn't understand was why he never called or stopped by after all we had done for him when he needed us the most. My entire family was heartbroken.

Corey had left me with nothing but lots of unanswered questions and even more confusion than I had before. I could still smell him all over my room and I often slept in his t-shirts to feel close to him. I had even reached out to Nu-Nu, however, she wasn't fucking with me anymore since I had broken things off with Nami. Here I was playing the role of the side dude hounding the girlfriend about her man.

After a while I assumed that Corey was never going to reach out to me and life had to go on…even without him. My family was experiencing some problems of our own.

I wasn't sure what was going on with my big sister, but she had us all concerned. Her mood was always so dark lately and she rarely smiled the way that she used to. Although only two years separated us, she had always been like a second mother to me. Now, she only spoke to us when she absolutely had to without getting her ass whooped by our parents. Well by mama, because our pops never laid a hand on Aimee. She had always been daddy's little girl.

Now she reminded me of Darlene from the show Roseanne. The majority of her clothing was black and her room was decorated with all black décor. It was scary. *She* had become scary. We all prayed that it was just a Gothic phase that would soon fade away. She was now in the twelfth grade and hung around odd looking people who acted and dressed much as she did.

Last week I had decided to stay home because I wasn't feeling well. I had been admitted to the hospital…yet again for four days. With it being Friday, I figured I'd just return to school on Monday. Mama had decided to leave me home alone since I had started feeling a little better. I finally climbed out of bed around eleven–thirty to heat up some leftovers when I heard a loud thump.

I had to clamp my hands over my mouth to stifle my startled scream. Grabbing a butcher knife, I slowly crept down the hall where I heard the noise. I reached my parents room first. Their bedroom door was open, and the coast appeared to be clear, so I kept it moving. Next, I reached Jonah's closed door. My heart was pounding as perspiration accumulated on my forehead.

Slowly turning the knob, I pushed his door open. I quietly exhaled when I realized that his room was also clear.

Taking a moment before continuing on my quest, I prayed to the good Lord that nothing crazy was hiding behind the next door. Standing outside of my sister's door, I noticed that it was slightly ajar. I quietly placed my face up to the crack and looked into Aimee's room. I literally lost my bowels at the sight before me.

Aimee was bent over on her bed, but she was not alone. My dear sister was stark naked with two overweight middle-aged men. One of them was drilling her from behind, while the other one pounded in and out of her mouth. The animalistic moans and the smell flowing through the air made me nauseous. I had to rub my eyes several times to ensure I wasn't trapped in a horrible nightmare. Unfortunately, every time my eyes refocused, the same images came into focus.

Their sickening activities came to a halt when I accidentally dropped the knife to the floor. It clanged loudly as I struggled not to throw up. Before I knew it, I had six terrified eyes glaring at me. Aimee appeared to relax once she realized it was *only* me. The guy that had been face fucking her, covered himself with her pillow, yet the fat fuck that was positioned behind her slowly resumed stroking in and out of her despite my presence.

"Hey Junior, I didn't know you were here. Close the door and I'll come and talk to you in a minute." Aimee stated.

All I could muster was a simple, "Okay," as I closed the door and retreated back to my bedroom. I wasn't even hungry anymore.

I sat on the side of my bed waiting for my sister to come and explain her actions for approximately thirty minutes. When she did come, she reeked of sex and appeared to be high as a kite. She appeared embarrassed as she slowly made her way into my room. As she attempted to plop down onto my bed, I quickly deaded that shit.

"Aimee, don't even think about sitting down on my bed! What the fuck is going on with you? You are letting old muthafuckas run trains on you now? What if it was mama or pops that had caught you instead of me?! What the fuck were you thinking, sis?!" I spat angrily with tears streaming down my face.

I had always looked up to Aimee, however, in that moment I was so disgusted and disappointed by her presence that I could've strangled her.

"Look Junior, I'm sorry that you had to see that. I'm going to keep it a buck with you. I started hanging around with this crowd at school last year and somehow they talked me into trying heroin with them. I knew that I shouldn't have tried it, but I didn't want to always be the party pooper. Anyway, I tried it for the first time this summer and I just can't shake this shit. I've tried bro, trust me. I don't like using the shit, but I just don't know how to stop Junior! Please don't tell anyone!" She broke down crying.

"No...Aimee no!" I wailed after hearing that she was abusing heroin. People like us didn't use drugs. How did heroin find its way to the Hilton household?

"That still doesn't explain why those two slovenly fat bastards were here." I naively stated.

"They are johns, Junior. They pay me for sex so that I can afford my drugs, but I'm sure they won't see me anymore after today. You spooked them and now they are afraid of being arrested for statutory rape."

"You're *sure* they won't be back?! Aimee please let me help you. You need to stop this or I will tell mama and pops!" I promised.

"I know, I know! Shit! I know that I need to stop. Each time that I use, I promise myself that each high will be my last. Do you think that I love living like this? All I think about is getting high. I hate what I've become Junior. Please try to understand. Don't betray me. I'll get help...I promise."

Keeping Aimee's secret was the most difficult thing for me to do. Every time I looked at her, I just wanted to tell our parents the truth. Her grades were in the toilet. She had become defiant and things began to disappear. It was hard seeing my mom thinking that she was losing her mind or simply misplacing things.

It all came to an ugly head after Aimee finally turned eighteen. My mom had us all searching high and low for her wedding ring. I was vexed with Aimee for the hell she had been putting our family through. After searching for the phantom ring for an hour, I decided that I'd had enough. Aimee hadn't been home in five days and since she was now legally an adult there wasn't anything my parents could do about it.

Walking into the living room, I sat my parents down and stated, "Mom...pops we need to talk."

"Sure son, what's eating at you?" My dad inquired.

"It's about Aimee. She is using heroin." I stated not beating around the bush.

"What the hell did you just say to us?!" My mother shrieked.

"She's addicted and is even selling her body and stealing things from the house to support her habit. I can't prove it, but I'm pretty sure she's taken your ring to get drugs. I'm sorry that I haven't told you sooner, but she manipulated me. She promised that if I kept her secret that she would stop using, but she hasn't! I am so sorry!" I cried.

While both me and mama bawled our eyes out, my dad looked as if he was having a heart attack. He was breathing heavily, and his face had turned bright red. Out of nowhere, he two pieced my ass. I quickly slid down onto the floor in a daze. I knew that I was lying on the floor, but at the time, I was unclear as to how it happened. Luckily, my devastated mother jumped in between the two of us.

"Get out the way Melanie! This little muthafucka knew my baby was out here using dope and didn't bother to tell us. He has been smiling in our faces every day while we try to figure out what is going on with her, yet he knew all along. He is about to take this ass whooping like a man, now move!" Dad growled.

"Merlon! I said stop it damn it! You cannot blame him for Aimee's mistakes. He was just trying to protect his sister. While it was poor judgment on his part, he didn't know any better. You and I both know how conning addicts can be. You better leave my child alone! Now get dressed so that we can go and find Aimee!" She screamed.

Finally finding my voice to speak again, I whispered, "I think I know where to find her."

Both of my parents' necks snapped in my direction as they glared at me.

"Well get your ass up and let's go and find my baby!" My dad boomed.

« Chapter 7 Cat And Mouse »

MY DAD MUST'VE BEEN driving one-hundred miles per hour to get to our destination. I was navigating him to a shady part of South Dallas. I only knew of this location because I've had to pick Aimee up a couple of times. Since her grades dropped and her attitude was so bad, our parents had confiscated both her cellphone and car.

Grim expressions swept over my parents' faces as we pulled up in front of the crack house I had the misfortune of entering a time or two in the past. The house had boarded up windows and random junkies scattered about the raggedy porch. I could smell the lead paint from the car. My dad looked at both my mother and I and told us to wait in the car. We both objected.

We were all going inside, besides I knew the room that she typically inhabited. Walking up the old steps, the fiends were like cockroaches begging for money to purchase their next hit with. The three of us were on a mission and heard and saw none of them. We were there for one reason and one reason only and that was to find and bring Aimee home.

Since I was familiar with the lay out, I led the way through the old dank two-story house. Upon reaching the top of the stairs that led to where I was sure my sister was, I glanced up and saw a young light skinned guy walking out of her room. We all looked on as he tossed a used condom onto the filthy ground and zipped up his jeans. My jaw dropped. I hoped that my parents didn't catch on, but I knew neither of them was stupid.

Luckily, they didn't know that he had just exited Aimee's room. Waiting for the guy to make his gleeful descent down the old creaky stairs, we continued on down the hall and into my sister's room.

Nothing about my sister really shocked me anymore, however, I prayed for my mom and dad's sake that she wasn't doing anything too shocking on the other side of the door. Taking a deep breath, I roughly pushed open the door.

The stench slapped us all in the face before the visual did. Aimee was lying on a thin filthy blanket on the ground completely nude. Her legs were still spread eagle from the sex that had just taken place moments before we arrived. Her pussy hadn't even had a chance to snap back and was still gaping open. She was high and was oblivious to our presence. Me and mama broke down again at the poor state my sister was in.

It was in that moment that I witnessed my father cry for the first time in my life.

It broke my heart to watch my dad place his face into his hands and cry his heart out. His shoulders shook violently as he processed everything that was going on.

"Why my baby? Why my beautiful baby, Lord?" He repeated over and over again.

Aimee looked so thin and smelled like a dead crackhead's pussy. I removed my jacket and wrapped it around my sister. My dad then picked her up off that odorous blanket.

The movement must've roused her a little because I heard her mumble, "Damn Q, you ready for another round already? Well, you know the price. No shorts today for this good shit."

My dad nearly dropped her as he snapped on her. "Aimee, wake the fuck up! This is your father!"

Those words appeared to instantly sober her funky ass up. Her eyes snapped completely open and she looked into each of our faces. Her eyes lingered on mine the longest as a look of disappointment came across her face.

"Look, you all can spare me the D.A.R.E speech. Daddy, just put me down and you all can leave. I'm not going anywhere with you! I'll come home in a few days. I'll get clean then." She lied.

"Oh God, how is it that I didn't see the signs sooner?!" My mom cried.

My dad simply ignored Aimee as he started walking back out of the room with her in his arms.

Realizing that my parents weren't going to be as easily manipulated as I had been, she yelled, "Daddy, I said put me down!"

Her weak attempts to wiggle herself free from our dad proved futile. By the time we reached the porch again she was screaming bloody murder. She was seriously trying to fight my dad until my mama slapped the taste out of her mouth.

Out of nowhere we heard, "Aye nigga, where do you think you are going with that bitch? I have four niggas who already paid me for her tonight. Put her ass back where the fuck you just got her from."

My father's glare was enough for the stranger to throw his hands up in surrender.

"She'll be back anyway. They always come back." With that he stormed off.

My mom decided to drive so that my dad could restrain Aimee in the backseat. We managed to get Aimee home. She was showered, fed and loved for three whole days, until she took off again. This cat and mouse game had become our life.

« Chapter 8 Where I Wanna Be »

IT WAS DEVASTATING to be powerless as Aimee fell deeper into her drug addiction. Our once picture perfect family was now tarnished. She had dropped completely out of school in her senior year and there wasn't a damn thing that any of us could do about it. Our family spent most of our evenings searching rundown crack houses for her. We had learned that she was now using any drug that she could get her hands on.

I had spotted her several times, but as the saying goes...it is impossible to catch a crackhead. I was number one on my school's track team, yet she always seemed to get away. My heart ached for my sister, but I didn't know what else I could do to help her. She didn't want our help, so after a while we had to accept defeat for the moment. We prayed that she would eventually grow tired of living the fast life.

My parents were both grieving and hurting for my sister. They were both stressed out and shells of themselves. My fifteen year old brother was obsessed with girls and seemingly had a different girlfriend every week. I still hadn't heard a peep from Corey, however, the word around our school was that Nu-Nu was pregnant with his baby. I started to truly hate that funky bitch. She was giving my boo something that I would never be able to.

Through all the chaos, I managed to do well in school. I focused on knocking my last few years of high school out of the way. I wasn't dating and didn't really have the desire to do so. Nami had forgiven me for the break up and we were now really good friends again. I continued to feign being straight and I hated it. I wished that there was someone who I could talk to, but there wasn't. The only person who I felt would understand my feelings had disappeared into thin air.

One day Nami called me up and asked me if I wanted to go to the town fair with her. It was super-hot out and I didn't really care for the rides. Of course, never being one to take no for an answer, she persisted and I eventually caved. Since confiscating Aimee's car, my parents had gifted it to me, so I agreed to pick Namiko up later on that day.

I spent the majority of the day reading an amazing book titled *My Wife's Daughters* by the dope author Sheena Perry. That book was bananas!!! You just can't trust anyone around your damn kids. Once I finished my book, I decided to hop in the shower. The warm water felt so good against my sore muscles. I had been practicing nonstop for an upcoming competition and today was my only off day.

Satisfied that I was squeaky clean, I took my time getting dressed. I opted to wear jean shorts and a plain white t-shirt. It was too hot for much else. I had just had my hair cut the previous day and I must say that I was looking like a snack. Once I was finished ogling over my own reflection, I grabbed my wallet and keys and headed out the front door. Nami only lived two minutes away, however, we were about thirty minutes away from the fair. I already knew parking was going to be a nightmare.

Upon pulling up to the festivities, my fears were confirmed. It was hot as hell and everybody and their mama was out there. I wanted to tell Nami that I'd drop her off and pick her up later, however, her excited squeals tugged at my conscience. I didn't want to flake out on her. I just couldn't bear to be the kill joy.

Nami looked beautiful as always. She was dressed in a form fitting pink summer dress and white sandals. The dress tied around her neck. Her typically bone straight hair now hung down past her shoulders in loose natural curls. She didn't need any make up, but I noticed that she had applied a little lip gloss to her already juicy lips. I don't know what swept over me, but I suddenly had a strong urge to kiss her and so I did. I actually expected her to stop me, however, she didn't.

She melted in my arms as I suckled on her tongue like a miniature dick. Pinching her hardened brown nipples through the thin material of her dress had me hard as a rock. I was ready to take her back home and push her walls aside for a few minutes. Almost as if she read my thoughts she pulled away from me and cleared her throat. I peeked at her from the corner of my eye as she straightened out her dress.

"Are you ready to go in, Junior?"

"Uhhh sure...lets go."

As soon as I paid our admission fee, the different food aromas instantly made my stomach growl. I hadn't realized that I had been so wrapped up into my book that I hadn't eaten anything all day. I guided Nami and myself towards the food stands. I purchased two chili cheese dogs, cheese fries, cotton candy, popcorn and a large sprite for myself. Nami ordered the nachos, a slice of pepperoni pizza and a coke. We were both small, but had ravenous appetites.

As we ate, we both people watched and talked about people as they walked by. I needed that and was happy that I had decided to come out after all. It was nice getting out of the house and not devoting my entire day to looking for my sister. After we scarfed down our food, Nami led the way through the crowd. Being the good sport that I am, I rode on just about every nauseating ride that she desired.

I was more of a ring toss sort of guy. She and I played, and I managed to win her an oversized pink bear. The damn thing was literally bigger than she was, and I was stuck with the task of toting that big, hot, hairy bitch around. Our overgrown asses got a huge kick out of the fun house. I hadn't laughed that hard in a long time.

Once we finished acting a fool inside of the fun house we stumbled upon a karaoke stage. We sat and watched a few people make fools out of themselves. After the fourth person performed Nami suggested that I get up there. A lot of people didn't know that I could sing, but I was pretty good. I could imitate just about anyone...male or female. By the time, the sixth person performed, I was amped and ready to do my thing.

I had opted to sing a male song as I did not want to come off as flamboyant in front of strangers, however, I typically preferred performing songs by women. I confidently walked onto the stage with a huge smile on my face. After introducing myself and announcing what song I had selected everyone was silently waiting for me to begin. Taking a deep breath I began.

I said I left my baby girl a message

Saying I won't be coming home

I'd rather be alone

She doesn't fully understand me

That I'd rather leave than to cheat

If she gives me some time

I can be the man she needs

But there's a lot of lust inside of me

And we've been together since our teenage years

I really don't mean to hurt her, but I need some time

To be alone

But when you love someone

You just don't treat them bad

Oh how I feel so sad

Now that I want to leave

She's crying her heart to me

How could you let this be?

I just need time to see

Where I wanna be

Where I wanna be

As I continued singing, I smiled internally as everyone cheered me on. They were truly taken aback by my voice and I was loving it. I sang that song better than Mr. Donell Jones himself. I don't think any of them were expecting such a huge voice from a scrawny teenage boy. At the end of the song, I was a little emotional because I felt every lyric in my soul. In a strange way, it reminded me of my relationships with both Nami and Corey.

Walking off the stage and back into the crowd I noticed that Nami was crying up a storm. She must've felt it too. I walked up to her and wrapped my arms around her. She wasn't necessarily who I wanted, but I did love her. I told her as much. We both decided that we'd had enough and were ready to head out. Unfortunately, out of nowhere my chili cheese dogs caught up to me. I had the worst case of the bubble guts ever! As I speed walked to the nearest restroom, I had to clench my ass to prevent its contents from seeping out.

Barely making it, I sighed in relief once I was able to spill the contents of my bowels into the toilet. My stomach cramped and contracted violently as large explosive acoustics reverberated throughout the stall. Sweat beads collected on my forehead as I promised never to eat another chili cheese dog ever again. Once I was finished, I felt a thousand times better. I washed my hands and walked out to find Nami still laughing at me.

Just as I was about to respond to her shenanigans, a familiar face came into view. Initially I didn't think too much of the familiar face until I looked down at the little light skinned, sandy haired boy in his arms. My eyes traveled from him to the petite caramel complexioned woman standing to his left side. I was in total disbelief as the enormity of the situation sank in. Just as I felt as if I had been kicked in my gut, his eyes met mine.

He looked as if he had seen a ghost. His already pale face had somehow managed to lose the little color it had. We stood completely still for what seemed like an eternity managing to ignore everything and everyone around us. Both Nami and his female companion wore confused expressions on their faces.

It wasn't until the little boy groaned, "Daddy! I have to pee pee!!!" That I snapped out of my trance.

"Really Pops!" I yelled before storming off into the crowd.

« Chapter 9 Family Man »

I WASN'T SURE WHAT WAS happening with our family, but I was almost certain that someone had put a curse on us. If it weren't for bad luck, we wouldn't have had any at all. Mama was devastated upon learning about my dad's other family. I gave him one day to come clean and confess everything after the fair incident. I told my father that if he didn't tell mama then I surely would. I couldn't believe that he would hurt mama like that. Him and Aimee were both now on my shit list for what they were doing to our family...to mama.

She was so depressed and had lost quite a bit of weight. She had kicked my pops out of the house and didn't want shit to do with him. He claimed that it was a onetime mistake that resulted in a pregnancy. He told mama that they weren't still sleeping together, but were simply co-parenting for the sake of three year old Marlon. That name was another slap in the face because it was too close to Merlon for comfort.

I was proud of mama for standing tall and sticking to her guns. My dad had pulled out every trick that he could think of, but mama wasn't taking the bait. She had been an incredible wife to my father, so I couldn't believe that he would throw everything away for a piece of temporary ass.

Jonah called himself being pissed at me for forcing our pops to come clean about his affair and love child. Jonah blamed me personally for our family's woes. He was on our father's side, of course. He couldn't fathom why mama couldn't just forgive our dad and mend our troubled family. He was much too young and immature to realize that it simply wasn't that easy. Our father was manipulative. He had started feeding Jonah sob stories to use to guilt my mother into taking our father back.

Approximately four months after my parent's separated, I was in the front yard cutting the grass when Nami ran up to me. She was talking so fast and was so excited that I could barely understand her. Shutting the lawn mower off, I asked her to repeat herself.

"I said Nu Nu is in the hospital about to have the baby!!! Can you take me up there to see her please?!" She sang flashing her vibrant pretty smile.

My girl couldn't get my dick hard to save her life, however, I could never resist her beautiful smile.

"Sure, Doll Face. Do I have time to take a five minute shower? I'm all sweaty and I have swamp ass babe." I stated seriously.

"Yes, but five minutes and that's it. I don't want to miss a thing!"

"Okay, here's my key. I'll be right back out." With that, I took off to the shower.

I was in and out of the house in twenty minutes and I was met by an irritated Nami.

"Baby, hurry up!!! You were in there for forever! You take longer than I do to get ready." She huffed with her arms folded across her small chest.

"I'm sorry. I tried to move as quickly as I could. You did spring this on me at the last minute!" I countered growing annoyed as well.

She blinked twice and I guess she thought about how foul she was coming at me and said, "You're absolutely right. I'm sorry for being pushy. I appreciate you for stopping what you were doing to bring me to the hospital."

Glancing at her I gave her tiny hand a gentle squeeze to let her know that all was forgiven. Honestly, I was still a little annoyed, but decided to suck it up and move on.

We rode the thirty minute commute in silence. I dropped her off at the entrance of the hospital and then went on the endless pursuit of trying to find a parking space that was within a ten mile radius. I lucked up and snuck into a nearby space for expectant mothers. I know I was wrong for that but fuck it, I was exhausted after cutting the grass.

Walking up to Nami who was waiting for me in the lobby, I burst into a fit of laughter once I saw her shaking her head. I knew she didn't approve of my parking choice. Her ass was going to have to get over it.

"What girl? I'm here to see an expectant mother aren't I?" I quizzed innocently.

"Boy, you are too much." Nami laughed.

We decided to make a quick pit stop at the gift shop to get Nu Nu a card, some balloons and some gifts for the baby.

Nu Nu had already given Nami the room number. The maternity ward was on the fifth floor. Once exiting the elevator, I was taken aback by how secure the unit was. While I'm no stranger to hospitals, I had never encountered anything quite like that before.

Upon reaching room 532, Nami gently knocked on the door. We heard Nu Nu yell for us to 'come in' and we obliged. As the hospital door swung open, my jaw dropped and my eyes bucked as I took in the sight of the boy I had grown to love. His very presence had me in a trance…only for a moment before I forced myself to compose myself. I didn't want to give him the satisfaction of knowing that everything within my being missed him.

There were days that I felt as if I couldn't breathe because I didn't know what became of him. How could he just disappear without so much as a text? Didn't he care about me just a little? The more I thought about how fucked up he had done not only me, but my family I grew more pissed.

My anger intensified when his inconsiderate ass nonchalantly glanced in my direction and offered me nothing more than a simple, "Sup."

I just nodded without a response. Prior to today, I had often fantasized about how we'd run into each other's arms after being apart for so long. This union was nothing like I had previously imagined. Why do our fantasies always have to be more blissful than reality?

Deciding to no longer give that heartless bastard anymore of my mental energy, I glanced at Nu Nu and smiled at her. She had her Poetic Justice braids pulled up on top of her head into a messy bun. Her pregnancy had her glowing. Despite her nose being wider than usual, she really hadn't changed much. At least not that I had noticed.

While Nami and Nu Nu discussed everything since they'd last seen one another…the day before, I took a seat and occupied myself with my phone. I completely ignored Corey, however, I could feel his eyes burning holes into me. After a while, I grew extremely exhausted and it was beginning to look as if their baby wasn't coming as soon as Nami thought. Nu Nu wasn't even dilated enough for an epidural, although she was in a lot of pain.

It was becoming difficult for me to keep my eyes open and I was getting hungry, so I announced to everyone that I was calling it a night. I told the ladies to keep me posted and promised that I'd return the next day. I didn't even bid Corey a farewell as I exited the room. Prior to getting on the elevator I decided to make a quick detour to the restroom. I couldn't recall the last time I'd used the restroom.

I relieved myself for what seemed like an eternity. As I opened the door to my stall, I was surprised when Corey pushed himself inside.

Sucking my teeth, I replied, "What the hell are you doing Corey? Get the fuck out of my way!"

He smiled, but didn't respond as he locked the door behind him and then proceeded to pin my arms above my head. I squirmed and wrestled under his grip. Although, I had missed the shit out of him, I was just too angry to just forget and forgive him so easily. As I half-heartedly fought to escape from his strong grasp, he pressed his lips onto mine and I just melted. I had no fight left. I couldn't even pretend to want him to stop anymore.

I felt so stupid for relinquishing all self-control that I had when it came to him. As I accepted his tongue into my mouth, I felt my wood stiffen. What was he doing to me? Why didn't Nami have such a powerful impact on me? Better yet, on my wood?

I felt weak in Corey's presence. I loved that boy with every fiber of my being. His strong touch brought tears to my eyes as I inhaled his Acqua Di Gio. By his flashy appearance and taste in cologne, I could tell that he had come into some money since I'd last seen him.

Feeling his erection press into my abdomen, I suddenly remembered why we were in the hospital and anger once again took over. I snatched away from his addictive touch and glared at him.

"Don't fucking touch me Corey."

"Nigga, what the fuck is wrong with your sensitive ass now?!"

"Bitch, I told you about calling me a nigga. Did you think shit was going to be all peachy between us after you just disa-fucking-ppeared? Wrong! Me and my family have been worried sick about you and your ungrateful black ass couldn't so much as call us to let us know that your crackheaded ass mama didn't kill you!"

"Watch your fucking mouth Junior. My mama has changed. I tried reaching out to you several times, I just didn't know what to say. A nigga was embarrassed about what we did in your room and shit. I didn't know how to face you. Then this baby shit..."

His last statement trailed off and stress took over his handsome face.

Looking at him made my glare soften. Although I was furious at him, I knew his life wasn't easy either. I had never considered what being a teenage father would be like for him. The sacrifices and changes were beyond my comprehension. One thing was crystal clear, I needed to get the hell away from him. Nothing good would ever come from our union. In the end, I knew he'd never be able to love me the way I needed and wanted to be loved. I'd always be his embarrassing dirty little secret.

A single tear escaped from my left eye as I pointed towards the door and whispered, "Go and be with your family C."

« Chapter 10 Cat Fished »

A YEAR HAD PASSED and I was still tolerating Nami. I truly didn't deserve her, however, she just couldn't let me go. I just couldn't shake her ass no matter how hard I tried. I couldn't be mean and break her heart, so I sacrificed my happiness for hers, yet again. While she mapped out our lives together and ranted about all the kids she thought we should have, I prayed for God to turn me into the man I knew she wanted me to be. I truly tried to make it work with her, but it was certainly forced.

I could never be myself around her. I always had to put on a super masculine persona in her presence, when I was internally as much of a diva as she was. I was that way around my father too. It was exhausting pretending to be someone I wasn't 24/7/365. I couldn't be myself around anyone except for...*him*. I actually hadn't had much contact with Corey. Honestly, I tried to avoid him at all costs. I knew I couldn't trust myself around him...my willpower was at a zero.

He and Nu Nu ended up having a baby girl named Shateara and naturally Nami was the Godmother. By default, I was crowned the Godfather and I took my title seriously. We spoiled that child rotten. In a way, I looked at her as if she were the child that Corey and I were supposed to have together, but were biologically unable to.

With all the love being showered over baby Shateara, her mother was notably absent. Corey and Nami had told me that her doctor had diagnosed her with a severe case of post-partum depression. Nu Nu refused to breast feed Shateara and rarely held her unless she was pretty much forced to do so. We all took turns caring for the gorgeous doll faced baby.

At times, I'd feel Corey staring at me on the few occasions we found ourselves alone, however, he knew better than to try me. I didn't have time for his confused, wishy washy ass. Either his big dicked ass wanted me all the time or he'd never have me at all.

In my spare time, I had started browsing dating sites looking for like-minded guys who wanted to hang out. I knew the internet could be dangerous and always felt that I was pretty cautious with the information I shared. I of course ran across the typical pervs and losers. I wasn't looking to hook up or for a friend with benefits relationship. I just wanted to meet guys around my age who were also experiencing confusing attractions to men. I couldn't discuss my feelings with the people in my life so I felt the only other solution was to meet complete strangers to confide in.

Out of the dozens of profiles I skimmed through, no one really caught my attention. Then one day, I received a notification that someone wanted to connect with me. The boy's profile name was DontAskDontTell420. His profile name told me that he most likely consumed marijuana. While I preferred to surround myself around drug free people, I didn't want to be judgmental. Weed was a gateway drug, but was it truly that bad???

After analyzing his name, I decided to click on the link that led to the message that he sent me. His pictures definitely caught my attention first. He was light skin with the juiciest lips I'd ever seen. His brown doe eyes were hooded by long lashes. His honey blonde tipped dreads were neatly styled in a variety of styles in his pictures. Shortly put, his ass was fine as hell! He was slim, but muscular.

After drooling over his pictures, I decided to check out his profile. According to his profile, he was nineteen…which was a little on the old side for me. He was a Christian. He was six foot three inches. He loved the colors black and yellow. Favorite food was Spaghetti and garlic bread. What baffled me was the fact that he listed that he didn't smoke or drink. After reading a little more about DontAskDontTell420, I finally read the message he'd sent.

DontAskDontTell420: *Hello LoveMeNot123, I read your profile and I think you seem like a cool guy. I would definitely like to get to know you better. You are sexy as fuck, but I know you get that a lot. I see that you're 17...will my age be a problem? I'm new to the area and trying to get to know some people like us in the area. No pressure. I'm cool with just being friends. BTW...I don't smoke weed. My birthday is 4/20. I hope to hear from you soon. If not, I know what time it is and wish you the best.*

Royce

It was that simple message that opened my heart to Royce aka DontAskDontTell420. I messaged him back two days after he sent his initial message so that I didn't come off as thirsty. We hit it off immediately and had all the chemistry in the world. We talked on the phone all the time and his deep baritone voice always took me over the edge when we had phone sex.

He was a little on the shy side and I just couldn't understand it because he was so sexy. Although, I had tried to link up with him several times, he was always so busy. Whenever he did agree to hangout, something would always conveniently come up. I couldn't even get his yellow ass to Facetime me. I tried to be patient and not be too pushy.

Nami could be pushy at times and it was such a turn off to me. Speaking of Nami, with Royce being in my life, it actually made being with her more tolerable. He would get me hot and bothered and in turn, I would deliver Nami the best sex of her life! I was tearing those walls to shreds. Our relationship and sex life had never been better.

On my eighteenth birthday my family and friends threw me a huge birthday bash. It was truly epic for several reasons. The first reason being I was able to track down and convince Aimee to sober up long enough to attend. Mama actually did a great job with cleaning Aimee up. Aside from being super thin, she almost looked like her old self again.

The second reason why this party was epic was because my parents were actually working on restoring their once troubled marriage. At first, I was completely against it and was pissed with my mother for caving and being weak. After lots of prayers, I finally realized that it wasn't my fight. Mama was lonely and she was so unhappy without my dad. No matter how much everyone tried to make her forget about our father, we were unsuccessful.

They attended marriage counseling twice a week to figure out where things had gone astray. Seeing my mom so happy because our family was under one roof again made my eighteenth birthday truly special. Our little brother Marlon was even in attendance, although, his home wrecking mama wasn't welcome. Some may consider mama weak for taking pops back and for accepting his lovechild, but this truly demonstrated and tested her strength.

My parents didn't hold back. They hired a DJ, had the food catered and decorated the hell out of our house for the occasion. We all danced, sang, ate and loved one another for hours. I was one lucky guy. I had a gorgeous woman on my arm who loved me through all of my imperfections. Well...almost all of them.

Despite having the time of my life, I knew the real fun was due to start after my party. Somehow I needed to figure out a way to ditch Nami. I had finally given Royce an ultimatum. He had been bullshitting me for nearly seven months and I was over it. I told him that if he flaked on my birthday then he had better lose my number. I was so excited about finally meeting my boo that I barely even noticed Corey. Corey looked and smelled like a snack as always, but I wasn't going there with him.

By mid-night the house was pretty much cleared out and Nami was passed out on our couch. I decided to creep upstairs so that I could freshen up and let Royce know that I was on my way over to his house. We'd been talking for nearly seven months at this point and I trusted him. After I got myself together, I hopped in my car and entered his address into my GPS. My stomach was twisting in knots as I anticipated this highly awaited union. I practiced what I'd say to him. I then became self-conscious and thought about all of my imperfections and hoped that he liked me as much as I liked him. Would I live up to his expectations?

By the time I pulled into the driveway of the address he'd given me, I had talked myself out of meeting my potential soulmate at least a dozen times. He was only thirteen minutes away from me, which actually annoyed me because of the time we wasted by not meeting sooner. Shrugging it off, I shot him a quick text letting him know that I was there and walking to his front door. I gave myself one last glance in my rearview mirror and headed to meet my prince at last.

Upon reaching the door, I rang the doorbell. I grew somewhat annoyed when I received a text stating to give him a couple of minutes because he was still getting dressed. I wasn't too pleased with having to wait, however, I wasn't going to allow that little detail to stop me from meeting my baby. Eight minutes went by and I was still standing outside looking like a fool. I decided to shoot him another text to see what the hell was going on. The long day of partying was starting to wear on me.

A minute later Royce apologized to me once again via text. He then told me that he was nearly finished dressing, and would have his "pops" open the door for me. I knew that Royce was a college student and still lived with his father. I replied with a simple 'okay'. He had told me that his parents shared custody of him for most of his life, but he'd always preferred staying with his father. His father knew that he was gay and was accepting while his mother was not.

Finally, I heard movement on the other side of the door. The locks clicked and the door swung open. As my eyes focused, I saw a tall light skinned man who looked just like Royce open the door. I could definitely tell that this was Royce's father. The most noticeable differences between the two men was the weight and the hair. His father had to be every bit of four hundred pounds. His dad also had dreads, but he had a large George Jefferson bald spot in the front of his head. It looked extremely silly to me. He would've looked much better had he simply went with a clean shaven bald look.

He looked very friendly and flashed me a huge welcoming smile.

"Hello sir. I am a friend of Royce. He is expecting me." I spoke politely extending my hand.

"Of course. Junior, right? That boy of mine talks about you all the time! Come on in and have a seat." He replied shaking my hand and then closing the door behind me.

"Thank you, sir."

"Oh, just call me Pops. Everyone does." He offered.

Glancing around, I took in my surroundings. There wasn't much furniture and there were roaches scattering all over the place. Old food and dishes decorated the cheap coffee tables. The smell was indescribable. I didn't want to come off as rude, but there was no way in hell I was sitting down anywhere. I told Pops that I was fine standing and that a drink wasn't necessary. He excused himself and I contemplated making a run for it. There was no way that I could be with someone who was okay with living in such filth.

Just as I was heading towards the door, Pops reentered the

living room holding a pistol. I don't know what came over me, but I instinctively ran for the door and turned the knob. Of course, it didn't budge. As I struggled with the locks, Pops or whatever the hell his name was walked up behind me and cold clocked me in the back of my head with his pistol. I think I was knocked out for a few moments, but not for too long. I remember being hoisted up and tossed over his shoulder. I've always been a small guy so I know his big ass didn't struggle much under my weight.

I remember whispering, "Where's Royce? Where's Royce?"

"I *am* Royce. Don't you recognize me baby? It's amazing what some old photos and a little Photoshop can accomplish nowadays. You don't know how long I've been waiting for this young tight ass." He bellowed as he firmly gripped my butt

His response shot chills up my spine.

With each heavy step his fat ass took, panic took over me. I think I feared lying on a filthy roach infested bed scared me more than being raped did. I had to come up with a plan to get my dumb ass the hell out of this mess...and fast!

He finally reached a foul smelling bedroom and I nearly threw up in my mouth as I glanced at the black cum stained comforter lying messily on the mattress in the corner of the small room.

He excitedly placed me back onto my feet and proceeded to pull his dick out of his zipper. I recognized his dick immediately and surprisingly he hadn't photoshopped his dick at all. It was long and thick and appeared to be freshly waxed. Seeing his swollen member, I knew exactly what I needed to do to save my ass...possibly my life too.

I licked my lips and seductively strutted towards Royce. I whispered in his ear that he didn't have to cat fish me because I thought he was sexy just the way he was. I then swiftly squatted in front of him, careful to steer clear of the roaches. I grabbed his supersized dick and began to stroke his meat. I watched in disgust as his predator-like head fell back and he began to thrust his pelvis into my hand. This went on for several minutes as I contemplated my next move. His pistol was still tucked firmly in his right hand. I had to be careful.

"Damn baby. I need to feel your mouth and then see those muthafucking cheeks jiggle soon. I've been waiting for this shit for way too long. Put it in your mouth really quick." He instructed matter-of-factly.

Me and his dick head were nearly eye to eye. His dick hole was so large and it almost appeared to be an empty eye socket blankly staring me in my eyes. I knew then that it was time for me to attempt my escape or die trying. There was one thing I was certain of...I was not putting that shit in my mouth.

Just as he prepared to repeat himself, I punched him in his humongous ball sack with all my might and hauled ass for the door. The floor shook as his large frame collapsed to the ground. At least I assumed it was his body. I didn't wait around to investigate. Once I made it outside of the room, I heard shots ringing out and pained cries coming from that room. Running as if I were on the track, I took off from the front door. This time I was able to successfully unlock the door.

I ran to my car so quickly that I don't even remember how I got there. I sped all the way to my house ensuring that I wasn't being followed. Luckily, as stupid as I was tonight, I was fairly smart in the larger scheme of things. Because Royce was coming off as so sketchy when it came to meeting and Facetiming, I had never told him my address, school or my real name. Essentially the only things I'd shared with him were two pictures and my phone number.

Once I reached my house, I quickly took another shower because I felt as if roaches were crawling on me. I then deleted all of the dating apps from my phone. Lastly, I skimmed through all of Royce's threatening texts prior to blocking his number. Maybe this was a sign from God that I needed to stick to dating women. Women weren't that crazy...were they???

« Chapter 11 Article 134 »

JUST AS THINGS HAD begun to calm down for my family, all hell broke loose once again. My dad's side chick, Geena was not pleased at all with his decision to work things out with my mom. I'm not sure what fairy tales she'd been told, but she was under the impression that she and my father were going to be together. It infuriated her that my father only wanted to co-parent baby Marlon with her and nothing else.

She first went after my father's wallet. She was requesting two thousand dollars per month in child support, which was ridiculous. She knew my parents made comfortable salaries and she felt that she was entitled to a piece of our American dream. It never ceases to amaze me how entitled bitches became just for spreading their sour ass pussies.

After making several court appearances, she was only awarded four hundred dollars a month in child support. I thought the bitch was going to stroke out when the judge read his verdict. This in turn resulted in her going after my father's military career. She had disclosed to his superiors that not only had my father, a military officer had an affair on his wife, but it resulted in a subsequent pregnancy.

Despite our soldiers having reputations for being whores, they actually have a strict adultery policy. Unfortunately for my dad, Geena was able to produce lots of incriminating evidence against him regarding their affair and illegitimate child. My dad's goal was to eventually retire after serving our great country for thirty years. Instead, he was dishonorably discharged under article 134. As a little luck would have it, he did not have to serve any jail time for his acts of indiscretion.

Who knew that my father's affair would lead to all of this?! I know for certain he didn't. I was once again infuriated with my father for embarrassing our family this way. One thing that I can say about my mama was she stood by her man through it all. When she decided to forgive him and give him a second chance, she meant it. Not once did I ever hear her throw his misfortunes in his face.

Since my father had been a high ranking Army Officer, he was making a substantial income. Now with him being dishonorably discharged, he was having a difficult time finding employment. He had been in the military for nearly thirty years and didn't have any other relevant work history. While he had managed to obtain a Bachelor's degree in Business while serving our country, it was essentially useless without a secondary degree to accompany it.

With my father being out of work and a four-hundred-dollar child support payment coming every month, mama was forced to pick up a second job. Her school nurse salary just wasn't cutting it. With her experience, she easily landed a weekend position at a prestigious children's hospital. I know she was exhausted from working two full-time jobs, but she never complained. I also landed a job at IHOP. I wasn't interested in helping my father out in any capacity, however, I didn't want to burden my mama any more than she was already.

The tips were enough to cover my basic needs. I knew that it was time for me to man up and figure out what I wanted to do with my life with graduation around the corner. For some reason I expected to feel different now that I was an adult, however, not much had changed. I was still in high school and I was still living with my parents. The two of them still dictated what I did and didn't do.

I wasn't sure what I wanted to do with my life, but people often told me that I should pursue modeling or acting. Maybe I'd major in theater. I needed to figure something out and sooner than later. I knew Nami loved doing hair, nails and makeup. She was going to cosmetology school as soon as we graduated. I supported her wholeheartedly and knew her ultimate dream was to own her own shop.

Ever since my birthday, Aimee had been trying to get her life together. She was currently in a rehabilitation center fighting for her sobriety. My parents had to take out a second mortgage on the house to afford it, however, Aimee was worth the sacrifice. I was so proud of my sister. Two days after my birthday, my mom decided to take Aimee to get a full physical because of the risky lifestyle she'd been living. Plus, she felt Aimee appeared sickly.

A week later, I overheard her telling my dad that Aimee had contracted gonorrhea and chlamydia while prostituting herself. None of that surprised me considering how she'd been living. What did surprise me was the fact that Aimee was five months pregnant. She claimed to not know. I visited her twice a week and with each visit a piece of her former self returned. I always brought her favorite strawberry French toast from my job. Her hair and skin glowed. I wasn't sure if it was from her being sober or if it was from her pregnancy.

Of course, she didn't have a clue as to who the father was. While none of us were particularly thrilled about her getting pregnant by an unknown john, this baby was nonetheless a blessing in disguise. Had she not learned of her pregnancy, she may not have decided to get her life in order. Her baby motivated her to strive for better. A pregnancy was a small price to pay in order to get my sis back.

∞

"Hey ma, I'm about to drop Shateara off at Nami's house. I'll be back in a minute." I yelled upstairs to my mom as I picked up my goddaughter.

Since Nami didn't live far and the weather was nice I decided to walk. It was nice watching the neighborhood kids outside enjoying themselves. It brought me back to my own childhood and how we'd have BBQs with our cousins. Things were so simple back then. Upon reaching the house it appeared that her parents were gone as the cars were missing. They never parked in the garage. Nami was afraid of driving and refused to learn so she didn't have a car.

Nami and her family rarely locked their back door, so I decided to try my luck. As always, I was able to walk right in. I'd warned her of the dangers dozens of times, however, it always went in one ear and out the other. I sat Shateara down on the couch and went to the fridge and grabbed a bottle of apple juice to pour into her sippy cup. I then diluted it with water to reduce her sugar intake. Turning the tv on, I found Cartoon Network and told her I'd be back with auntie Nami.

I jogged up the stairs ready to be relieved of my godfatherly duties. I loved her dearly, but she was at that age where she required constant supervision. I was exhausted. We tried to alternate weekends between me, Nami and Corey. Nu Nu was still uninterested in being a mother. Shateara had an appointment in the morning and Nami's mother agreed to take, her which was why I was dropping her off early.

Once I reached her door, I twisted the knob. I could hear a male whispering, but I could not determine what he was saying. By this time I was twisting the knob with one hand and banging on the door with the other.

"Hold on a second, mom." I heard Nami call out.

I had decided not to say anything because I knew that she'd never open the door if she knew that it was me on the other side. I heard scuffling going on in her room. I was so pissed that I could feel steam seeping through my ears. I had stopped banging because I didn't want to alarm Shateara downstairs. When the door finally swung open, a surprised Nami appeared in front of me. She looked as if she'd seen Candyman. I scowled at Nami and my eyes scanned her bedroom. I was no fool, I heard a male voice.

Brushing past her, I speed walked to her closet door. I immediately noticed that her bed was a mess, which wasn't like Nami. She was the tidiest person I knew aside from mama. I also noticed the distinctive smell of sex permeating the air. There weren't too many places to hide in her room and I am speaking from experience. Either this clown was in the closet or he was hiding his simple ass under her bed. Nami was on my trail as I snatched open her closet door.

As I began moving items aside, she yelled, "Junior! What the hell are you doing?! What are you looking for? You are acting crazy. I would like for you to leave now."

I couldn't help but to let out an amused laugh as her words sunk in. She had never asked me to leave before. In fact, she was always in her feelings whenever I attempted to leave. This further added to my suspicions.

Seeing no signs of life within her large walk in closet, there was only one other place to look. Brushing past her petite frame once again, I headed over to her bed. She went into full panic mode once she realized I wasn't leaving.

"Junior! I told you to leave! Get the hell out of my house acting crazy!!! Don't make me call the police." She threatened.

I didn't bother responding to her. I was going to leave just as soon as I peeked under her bed. Just as I was about to kneel down, I heard a familiar voice say, "Aight nigga you found me. Now what?"

My mouth flung open as soon as I saw Vasti's chimp-like face peer from under Nami's bed. I was so disappointed and disgusted that I literally vomited all over Nami's floor which simultaneously splashed on Vasti. She knew that Vasti and his crew were my number one enemies. While looking at Vasti as he struggled to get up so that he could whip my ass, the logical side of me kicked in.

I lived by a simple principle. Never fight an ugly person with nothing to lose...aesthetically speaking. Any punch that I landed on him would have certainly been an improvement to homeboy's vomit covered face.

"I hope your enjoying my mama's homemade chili muthafucka." I seethed peering down at him.

I walked up to a mortified Nami, kissed her on her forehead and told her that Shateara was downstairs.

Before running out of the room, I looked her in her eyes and said, "Thank you."

Surprisingly, I meant it.

« Chapter 12 Meelah »

ALL MY LIFE I FELT as if I had to put on a macho act to appease my father. It killed me to have to suppress my desire to wear makeup and dresses. My mind would often drift back to how my dad had beaten the hell out of me and then cut my hair off when I was a small child. Despite my pathetic attempts to be the straight man that my parents had raised me to be, I knew it was all in vain.

Two weeks after I had caught Nami and Vasti fucking, I was doing everything in my power to dodge them both. Obviously, I was avoiding Vasti and his crew because he wanted to whoop my ass for throwing up on him that day. Nami...now that bitch was persistent! I never told my family why she and I had parted ways, so naturally they assumed that it was my fault.

She showed up and called relentlessly, however, we had absolutely nothing to discuss. We were over and done with. Truth be told, we were over prior to me catching her, I just didn't have the heart to break hers. Unbeknownst to her, she had finally given me my out after years of being held captive. I was sick of pretending to be someone I wasn't. Why couldn't I be myself? Was I so bad?

I was in the midst of wrapping up my senior year and deciding on what I wanted to do upon my graduation. I had asked my friend, Meelah to accompany me to the senior prom. Meelah's name suited her perfectly as she bore an uncanny resemblance to the 702 singer Meelah. She was a chocolate covered beauty. She was in between boyfriends and well...you know how my situation with Nami played out.

Meelah had talked me into growing my hair out a while ago so that I could sport braids. She was a beast when it came to braiding. I hated the transitioning phase, but now that I had a decent length of hair I was feeling it. She and I had started hanging out a lot during our senior year and I enjoyed her company. She initially didn't know that I was into men because I hid it so well. I eventually came clean and told her the truth. I even told her that I was still in love with Corey.

I don't know, why but I was able to confide in her with just about everything. She was so open, honest, bold and hilarious. Meelah and Nami had never gotten along and I never really understood why. I suppose Nami felt threatened by Meelah. Nami obviously didn't understand that I wasn't sexually attracted to either of them. After I discovered that Nami was cheating on me, Meelah wanted to whoop her ass in my honor.

I told her to just let it go. Hell, her acts of indiscretion freed me. I was off the hook. She told me that she owed her an ass whooping anyways for the times that she'd come at her sideways. Nami was notorious for throwing shade at Meelah. As much as I knew Meelah wanted to connect Nami's face with her fists, she refrained herself out of respect for me. She knew that if she fought my then girlfriend that it would've caused issues within our friendship. She was definitely a class act, but she was no pushover either.

We had a little over a week before prom and I wanted to make sure that everything was together. Although the prom wasn't a huge deal to me, it was for Meelah and both of our mothers. I had just received a call notifying me that the alterations for my tux were complete and that I was free to pick it up. Meelah wanted us to both wear baby blue and white and so we were.

On my way to pick up my tux, my gas light went off.

"Damn it!" I yelled.

Every time I sat behind the steering wheel that fucking car needed something! Before I got too far away from home, I pulled into my favorite QuikTrip. While pumping gas, I had my music blaring Pour It Up by Rihanna. I was singing my heart out while making a feeble attempt not to twerk. The gas station was busy as usual and you never knew who was watching. The pump clicked indicating that my tank was once again full. As I reached to remove the nozzle, I felt warm breath on the back of my neck followed by a hard object being pressed into my back.

I then heard a deep baritone voice whisper, "If you scream, I'll blow your fucking brains out! Now turn around slowly." It creeped me out so much, but as badly as I was afraid to spin around, I was even more afraid not to.

Spinning around slowly, I prayed to God that he allowed me to escape from this situation. Who the hell would be robbing me in broad daylight on a busy ass gas station's parking lot?! This world simply had no chill. Well the final joke was on this muthafucka because all I had on me was eight dollars after filling up my gas tank. My debit card was conveniently stashed inside of the inner console of my car. As I slowly spun around, I began to explain that I only had eight dollars when the robber's face came into view.

"Awwww, man! Jacoby, you play way too much!!!" I whined as I slapped Jacoby on his arm.

Jacoby was one of the cooks from my job at IHOP. He was

Puerto Rican and black. If I were to say that he was gorgeous…that would be an understatement! He had a beautiful bronzed complexion with jet black hair. His eye brows were naturally arched to perfection and he had the darkest blackest pair of eyes that I had ever seen in my life. They were so piercing that it appeared as if he could see right into my soul.

In that moment I couldn't have cared less about how sexy he was. I wanted to karate chop him in his throat for raising my blood pressure the way he had.

"Sup Junior. What are you doing in my neck of the woods?" He asked.

"I'm just running a few errands since I had a half day at school. What are you up to? Are you off today?" I quipped still trying to get my breathing and temper under control.

"Yeah, I'm off today. I was just headed to Forest Park to shoot some hoops. Wanna come?"

"No, I'm straight." I declined trying to sound cool.

"Nigga, that ain't what I heard." He replied.

"What?! Man Jacoby, fuck you! Get the hell out of my way." I shrieked brushing past him.

Damn, he smelled good I thought as I hurriedly got into my car to put distance in between the two of us.

He simply stood there with an eerie smirk on his face. I gave his sexy ass the middle finger before I sped off to my next destination.

Little did I know, that pretty son of a bitch was about to turn my world upside down!

« Chapter 13 Blackmail »

PROM CAME AND WENT, but of course not without a little drama. Meelah and I were having the perfect evening living our best lives without a care in the world. She looked stunning in her baby blue and white strapless form fitting dress. None of the other girls in the room held a candle to my bestie. We both loved to dance so we spent the majority of the evening grinding as she twerked her ass all up on me. The music alternated between 90's hits and contemporary music.

I thought Meelah was going to pass out once we were crowned King and Queen. Couldn't no one tell my girl shit that night. We had both noticed Nami and Vasti there together. They both appeared to be watching us all night. Nami had a scowl on her face and did not look as if she even wanted to be there. Corey and Nu Nu had made a quick appearance, however, I hadn't seen either of them for quite a while. I assumed they dipped out to be with Shateara.

At some point as both Meelah and I were talking about calling it a night, I heard Nami yell, "See, I knew that I didn't like your hoe ass for a reason! You just couldn't wait to take my man from me! Junior, did you really choose this crispy bitch over me?!?!"

Just as I was about to respond, I watched in horror as Meelah eight-pieced Nami in rapid succession, dropping her instantly. Meelah had those hands and my bitch was fast as hell with them too!

By this time, we were completely surrounded by the nosy ass students and our annoyed teachers. Nami was still laid out when Vasti came over trying to fight me. Luckily, several people grabbed him, and he was immediately escorted off the premises. While the teachers attempted to rouse Nami, I told Meelah that we better book it. I prayed that my friend didn't get into too much trouble. Luckily for her, if Nami woke up and decided to press charges, she was still seventeen and wouldn't be tried as an adult. Nami was eighteen on the other hand.

As crazy as our prom night turned out, it was a night that I'd never forget. Nami did end up pressing charges against Meelah. She spent three days in juvie and was on house arrest until her eighteenth birthday, which was three months away.

When asked if it was all worth it, her response never wavered, "Hell yes, it was worth it! And bitch I'd do it again! I want to knock her snooty ass out every time I see her! She talks all that shit, but can't fight."

A week later while wandering aimlessly down the never-ending aisles of Walmart, my phone rang. I did not recognize the number, however, unlike most people, I always answered my phone. Hell, I was still too young for debt collection calls!

"Hello?" I spoke in a questioning manner.

"Yo nigga, what's up?" The familiar voice responded.

"Corey, how many times do I have to tell your ugly ass to stop calling me that?! Secondly, why are you calling me from this weird number and lastly where is my goddaughter?"

"Why are you always whining about being called a nigga, man? It's a word I use for people that I'm cool with. You need thicker skin. Man up a little, nigga. It's much different than being called a nigger. To answer your second question, this is my new number, so save it. Shateara is with Nami today. It's her week with her. But that isn't why I called you." He stated, but failed to elaborate.

"Well what the hell did you call for then?" I snapped growing impatient with his shenanigans.

"I saw you the other day talking to Jacoby..." He paused.

"Yeah...and?" I mumbled sarcastically while rolling my eyes.

"Ummm, well stay away from him Junior. He's bad news for real man." He stammered.

I found it cute that he was having such a difficult time conveying this message. He was always such a straight forward and blunt person.

"How is he bad news Corey?" I inquired.

"Just trust me on this, alright? Stay the fuck away from him!"

"Muthafucka, I know you aren't..." I glanced at the phone to verify what I already suspected and saw red when it was confirmed that his bitch ass had hung up on me.

I called him back three times in a rage and he quickly sent my angry ass to his voicemail each time. Don't think for a second that I didn't light into his ass each time via his voicemail after each beep. I don't know who the fuck he thought he was to tell me not to talk to someone. He wasn't my daddy, nor was he my zaddy! If I didn't know any better, I'd swear that ole' Corey was a little green.

His immature warning and apparent jealousy had peaked my curiosity. While Jacoby was sexy as hell, I wasn't interested in a romantic way. Plus, I didn't like how our little conversation went at the gas station. Much like Corey, he was a little too arrogant and cocky for me. I wanted someone a little more on the humble side. Corey was still the love of my life, but I was sick of waiting for his ass to *"see"* me. Not necessarily in a physical way, but more so metaphorically.

Now that he'd let me know that he wanted me to steer clear of Jacoby, I was going to make it my business to get to know him a little better. During our upcoming shift together, I was going to make sure that we exchanged numbers. Corey had me fucked up!

∞

Over the next couple of months, Jacoby and I hung out as much as we could. It was nearing the end of my senior year and we both worked a lot. He turned out to be pretty cool. He was twenty-two and had his own spot. The only thing I didn't like was the fact that he had three kids with three different women. I tried not to allow it to bother me too much since he never had them over when I visited. He didn't make much at IHOP, however, I knew he sold bootleg DVDs and body oils to supplement his income.

Of course no one knew that we were dating because neither of us was out. We never did anything too special. Our dates primarily consisted of me hanging out for a couple of hours. We basically netflixed and chilled. I never brought him over to my house because of the lack of privacy. I knew my parents would question why his old ass was hanging around a high school student...although I was technically an adult myself now.

Of course, he tried to fuck me every time we were together, but I just wasn't ready. Plus, I wasn't sure if he was who I wanted to give myself to the first time. I know it sounds like a cliché, but I really wanted my first time with a man to be special. I wanted it to be with Corey, but he was still on bullshit with his confused ass. I suppose Jacoby was too, but I wasn't in love with him, so it really didn't matter.

A few days after I had graduated...with honors I might add, Jacoby had offered to treat me to a celebratory dinner. While I was small, I loved to eat and wasn't about to turn away a free meal. I don't know how he was able to afford it, but he'd somehow managed to get us reservations at Da Marco. From what I'd heard it was always booked. We both were adorned in fancy suits and looked flawless. It was difficult pretending to be platonic because I felt so special in that moment that I wanted nothing more than a make out session with Jacoby.

He had certainly outdone himself with that dinner. No one had ever made me feel as special as he did that evening. I didn't know what half of the shit was on the menu, so I stuck with Chianti braised short ribs. Jacoby was a little more adventurous and ordered the Australian lamb loin with cumin yogurt. When our entrées arrived, I was all but salivating at the sight and smell of my food. His looked good, however, mine looked better.

We talked about just about everything and I felt safe and happy with him. For the first time, I contemplated giving up on Corey and pursuing something real with Jacoby. He was really stepping up and I was certainly impressed. I wasn't sure what lie ahead in my future, but I was almost certain that I wanted Jacoby to be a part of it.

After dinner, Jacoby asked if I wanted to go to his place for a little while. Of course, I told him yes. He'd just spent a small fortune on one meal when I knew his pockets weren't that deep. I never wanted the night to end. On the way over to his place I noticed him checking his phone and periodically texting. I hated when people texted and drove, and he knew that. I bit my tongue because I didn't want to ruin the mood.

I guess he noticed the change in my facial expression and apologized. He claimed it was one of his kid's mothers' asking him to drop off some money the following day. He then put his phone down and commenced to focusing on the road.

We arrived at his house and I immediately began kissing him. Our breathing was labored and my pipe was stiffer than a corpse. I still couldn't say whether or not I was in love with Jacoby, but I definitely had strong feelings for his sexy ass. Our eyes locked onto one another as we swiftly removed our suits. My mouth watered as his ten inch dick sprang into view. I immediately dropped to my knees and began working my jaw muscles. I wasn't sure if my mouth was capable of accommodating his girth, but I was soon about to find out.

I first stuck my tongue out ensuring that it was covered in saliva. I flicked the head of his penis as I grabbed a hold of his clean shaven balls. I took my tongue and trailed it lightly down the length of his tool. I knew I must've been doing something right because his head was back as if he was looking into the heavens. Once I found my comfort zone, I opened my mouth up wide and slowly inched his sex organ down my throat like a snake swallowing its prey.

I was apparently a natural as I engulfed him completely without even the slightest gag. I was enjoying pleasing him to the fullest. Spit was dripping down my chin by the gallons. I hummed and moaned loudly to emphasize how much I was enjoying my dessert. I watch as he squirmed around like a bitch unable to contain his pleasure.

Finally, he snatched his dick out of my mouth and stated, "Damn Junior, are you sure you never did that shit before?! Your head game is official!"

"I aim to please. I'm glad you enjoyed yourself." I said feeling myself.

He smacked me on my ass and instructed me to follow him to his bedroom. I obliged.

I hadn't ever been inside of his bedroom outside of quickly grabbing something for him. I tried to avoid it so that he wouldn't get any wild ideas. I guess tonight was going to be the night in which we explored all of those ideas. I silently prayed that we both lived up to each other's expectations. I know that he'd been waiting for a long time and I didn't want to disappoint him. I'd been waiting eighteen years for this very moment and I sure as hell didn't want to leave unsatisfied.

Once we reached his room, I stared at him sheepishly. His dark eyes studied my body intensely. Starting to feel self-conscious, I reached for his comforter to cover up with, but he stopped me.

"No, don't do that. You're perfect Junior. I'm taking the sight of you all in. How in the fuck did I get so lucky?"

I blushed as I released the comforter. He walked over to me and gently pushed me back onto the bed. My bravery went out the window as the magnitude of what was about to transpire sunk in. Was this shit really about to go down? Right here? Right now? Jacoby was on top of me in an instant. He kissed me as he grinded his pelvis into mine. Both of our erections were stabbing at one another. It was then that I realized that he wasn't much into foreplay. I was expecting some head in return or for him to eat the groceries…or something!

I watched as he walked over to his nightstand and retrieved a golden wrapped condom. He hurriedly applied it and seductively smiled at me. He then placed a pillow under my hips, hacked up a loogie and expelled it onto my asshole. I felt his finger as he smeared it around. Satisfied with his natural lubrication, I stiffened up as I felt him begin to head fuck me. The pain tore through my body and paralyzed me.

"Ssssssss oh God!!!" I hissed loudly.

I was expecting pain, but I wasn't quite expecting for it to be this intense. I wanted to stop and was about to tell Jacoby as much, but when I looked up into his face, I felt guilty for not being able to take the pain. He was on top of me with his eyes closed in pure bliss. I just didn't have the heart to tell him I'd changed my mind. Instead, I tried to breathe and scream my way through the pain. I was certain that if his neighbors didn't know his name before, they knew it now.

As Jacoby finally worked all of his inches into my ass, I held my legs up praying that he'd cum soon. We were both covered in sweat and all I knew was my asshole was on fire. How did people do this shit…and actually like it? Finally after what felt like hours, he finally stiffened as he sexually grunted and I felt his stick pulsate within my backdoor. I watched in horror as he withdrew his softening dick from my sore opening and the condom was covered in my virginal blood.

As I lay there, I questioned many things, my sexuality being one of them. Maybe homosexual sex wasn't for me. I didn't like it even remotely. I knew then that I wasn't doing that shit again…or so I thought. I was in too much pain to even move, but I knew I needed to get home so that mama didn't worry. Just as I completed that thought, three unfamiliar dudes came barging into the bedroom. I hadn't even realized that Jacoby had even left the room after ripping me a new asshole.

I sat up immediately and covered myself the best I could with the blue comforter beneath me. I was afraid that we were about to get robbed and possibly murdered because we'd been discovered in the aftermath of our homosexual dalliance. I wasn't sure where Jacoby was, but I hoped those hoodlums hadn't caused him any harm. I glared at each of their faces studying and memorizing every detail that I could, so that I could identify them in a lineup for whatever crime they were about to commit.

Out of the three men, only one was attractive. They never spoke, they just looked at me, but I wasn't sure why, so I decided to break the ice.

"Look, I don't know why you're here, but I don't want any problems. I have a little over one-hundred dollars in my wallet. It is over there in my suit jacket."

Neither of the men even blinked to acknowledge they'd even heard me. Just as I was about to reason with the men again, Jacoby returned unharmed and unfazed by the presence of the three men. I assumed he must've known them so hopefully they weren't here to harm us.

"Jacoby! Do you know these guys? If so, why are they in here just staring at me? This shit is a little strange." I asked feeling a little better because of his calm demeanor.

I watched as Jacoby went over to my suit jacket and confiscated the money from my wallet. He then transferred it into his own wallet, which he had placed on his nightstand.

"That will replace the money I spent on your greedy ass tonight." Jacoby stated coldly.

I wasn't sure what was going on, but a feeling of foreboding consumed me. I knew that something horrible was about to happen and I also knew that it was beyond my control.

"Junior, I'm sure you're a little curious as to what is going on aren't you?" Jacoby asked with a serious expression on his face. He looked as if he had no soul. His dark eyes were pitch black now.

I simply nodded without saying anything.

"Well, here's what is happening, I sell sexual services to those in need. And currently these fellas are in dire need.

My eyes grew wide. My mouth went completely dry and my breathing became erratic. This couldn't be happening right now. I had just finished having sex with a man for the first time ever and just minutes later I was about to get raped by three men. I knew I'd never survive that torture again. They were just going to have to kill me because I wasn't going through that pain three more times when I felt as if I had already been split in two.

As if reading my mind, Jacoby finished. "Now I am *NOT* in the business of raping people. I've never done that and never will. All of my workers do so willingly. With that in mind let's watch this quick little video for a second…shall we?"

I responded by sitting up higher so that I could watch whatever video he felt the need to show me. I watched Jacoby fumble around for a few moments before my eyes bulged out of their sockets. That sneaky bastard had secretly recorded the sex that we'd just had. I had never felt more humiliated in my life. The three guys stood there patiently as they too watched my screaming and moaning in pain. Luckily, you couldn't see either of our faces well due to the shitty angle and the quality of the camera.

"You son of a..." I yelped as I tried to make it over to him, but pain shot in my rectum so I slowly sat back down.

I guess Jacoby felt that I'd had enough and cut the video off. He then directed his attention back to me.

"So Junior as I was saying, I do not force people to have sex. After watching their little movies, they are usually begging to work for me. Think about all the havoc that can be brought about if your video lands into the wrong hands. Let's get to the point, you will work for me. You will be on call twenty-four hours a day and I will keep sixty percent of the profits for one year. You will then be released from your duties. That is, unless you wanted to continue working for me. You have my word."

"And what if I refuse?" I asked defiantly.

"Then I will make your ass a celebrity overnight on Pornhub. Your friends and family will all get their personal copies." He replied matter-of-factly.

My heart sank. Tears grazed my cheeks as I weighed the pros and cons of both options. I honestly thought Jacoby gave a fuck about me, but I guess I was mistaken. I was internally scolding myself for not heeding the signs staring me in the face. I should've gone home directly after dinner and this would have all been avoided. I thought long and hard for several minutes before I came to a conclusion.

One of the three guys finally interjected irritably.

"Yo Jacoby, is this shit happening tonight or naw? I have shit I need to take care of and this little scary nigga is holding us up man. Let us know so that we can get our money back."

They had the audacity to speak about me as if I weren't right there in front of them.

Jacoby looked nervous as he glanced in my direction with pleading eyes.

"So what's it going to be Junior?"

"I've decided that I am not going to work for you so do what you feel is necessary. I'm not about to sell my ass for you or anyone else!" I shouted with a false sense of bravery.

"Are you sure about this? You better think about this and be smart nigga. What will your folks say about our little flick?" Jacoby attempted to persuade me.

"I told you where I stood. If you all don't mind, I'll be going now." I said firmly while grabbing my clothes.

I quickly put my clothes on and then shot Meelah a text asking her for a ride since I didn't drive to Jacoby's house. She didn't live far and told me that she'd be there in five minutes. It was hot as hell, yet I'd opted to wait for her outside. I had to get away from Jacoby and those other fuckers who thought they were about to get their dicks wet.

As I waited in front of Jacoby's apartment I broke down sobbing. I couldn't believe that such a perfect night had ended so badly. I should've listened to Corey when he told me to stay away from Jacoby. I thought he was just speaking from sheer jealousy, however I now knew there was more to his warning.

I quickly wiped my face as the three guys exited the apartment and headed to their vehicles. They lustfully mugged me on their way. Jacoby stood on his porch glaring angrily.

"You have no idea how much money you've just cost me. You are going to pay for this nigga."

Meelah pulled up at that very moment. I looked at Jacoby one last time and said, "Fuck you and everything you stand for. Stay the fuck away from me and my family bitch!"

With that I got into my bestie's car and never looked back.

« Chapter 14 Homo-Hetero »

MY PARENTS WERE IN a good place for the first time in a long time. My dad had found a job working as a security guard at a nearby grocery store. It was nowhere as desirable as his military position, however, it helped foot the bills. Mom was able to cut back on her rigorous work schedule at the hospital a little now that my father was contributing again. I had noticed that his self-esteem had plummeted after being discharged from the military. It was nice seeing that being restored.

He took great pride in his job and was happy to be given a second chance with us all. I had put all of my anger and resentment aside for my pops because I could see he was truly trying. Geena was being the typical bitch and doing everything in her power to keep my father away from Marlon. She was the most vengeful person I'd ever encountered. She still tried everything in her power to get my father to leave my mother. Whenever he would turn down her advances, she'd punish him by denying him access to Marlon.

We had all gotten to know and love the newest member of our dysfunctional family. After playing the cat and mouse game with Geena for a while enough was enough. My parents knew their rights and since my father was listed on the birth certificate and was paying child support there was no reason why we should not be a part of Marlon's life. After several court appearances, my dad was awarded joint custody of Marlon. This also stopped the four-hundred dollar a month child support payments. Each parent was responsible for the child's care and expenses while under their own care.

To say that Geena was furious would've been an understatement. She had defied the court's order once by refusing to release Marlon over to my dad and my parents made an example out of her ass and had her arrested. We didn't have a problem with that anymore. It took a little time for everyone to adjust to the changes, but we were slowly progressing as a family. My sister was sober and was back to her old self. She was so beautiful and very pregnant. Despite the circumstances surrounding her pregnancy, I couldn't wait to meet my little niece. I was going to spoil her rotten just like I did Shateara.

We had all pitched in and bought the baby essentially everything she'd need, but we still wanted to throw her an official baby shower. Aimee spent the majority of her days nesting and ensuring things were in order for baby Skyy. It was still hard to believe that in eight short weeks my big sister was going to be a mama. With our help, she planned to follow in mama's footsteps and go to nursing school. She had the best teacher in the world, so why not? Aimee was compassionate and had a heart of gold when she wasn't getting high, so I knew she'd make an amazing nurse.

Jonah was the typical teenage boy. He preoccupied most of his time with video games, music, girls, sneakers and sports. He was a good kid overall. He was definitely dad's favorite…Aimee had fallen to second place after her drug addiction.

It had been a month and Jacoby continued to hound me to come and work for him. He had tried damn near every tactic known to man to coax me, but I wasn't having it. The fool even tried to convince me that he cared about me and wanted to start over. He was sicker than I thought. I knew he was bluffing about sharing that video. Honestly, I wasn't too concerned about it because as I said before the quality was so shitty that you really couldn't tell who was in the video unless you knew our voices.

"Damn boo, you are looking like a snack tonight!" I told Meelah as we got ready to head out to a club called 5th Amendment. Meelah's chocolate skin was radiating as usual and required very little makeup. She sported a yellow form fitting dress that was all sheer in the stomach area and lower back region. Her tight six pack was visible which even made my sweet ass drool a little bit. I glanced down and noticed that she was sporting the black Jimmy Choo heels that I'd gotten her as a graduation present a few months back. Her finger and toenails were painted yellow as well.

Her silk wrap was styled to perfection as her natural hair reached her mid-back. Walking behind her, I bent her over her bed and humped on her ass like a dog in heat. She laughed before she spun around and playfully pushed me away.

"Junior, get your crazy ass out of here before I put this pussy on your sideburns!" She joked copying one of Nicki Minaj's infamous lyrics.

"Bitch please, sideburns aren't even in style. Plus, I couldn't help myself. You look so good that you turned me straight for about twenty seconds! I was about to dive into that gushy stuff, fish!" I half joked.

I would totally lay the pipe down on my friend in a heartbeat and she knew it. I also knew that I could get her too, but neither of us had crossed that line. I knew that it would be a huge mistake on my end because of my love for men. I had told Meelah about the situation with Jacoby, but she too called his bluff. She thought he was just trying to strong arm me into getting what he wanted. She had to remind me that he was in the closet too and wouldn't expose himself as he too was in the video.

Why hadn't I thought about that before?! It made perfect sense and I thanked the Lord above that I hadn't allowed those guys to run through me.

"Junior, did you hear me?" Meelah asked with concern etched into her pretty face.

"No, sorry. What did you say?" I answered.

"I asked if you were ready to go. I'm ready to go and shake my ass bih!!!" She squealed popping her round ass within dick's reach.

I stood behind her and playfully smacked her on her round ass until her silly ass nearly fell face first onto the floor.

"Let's go girl. You're driving tonight!"

The club was packed! The line was longer than an old lady's tits, but we waited anyway. I felt bad for Meelah because she had to endure the wait in six inch heels. We finally made it in after a thirty minute wait. I was so excited because I had never been to a club before. It was pretty dark, yet still light enough to see what the club had to offer. The DJ was on point too as he played a little bit of everything. They certainly catered to our diverse community.

Neither of us were old enough to drink, so we avoided the bar area. Instead, we headed straight for the dance floor. The Migos Walk It Talk It began to play and we both squealed excitedly. That was our shit! As badly as I wanted to twerk like Meelah, I had to maintain my composure. I was still uncomfortable with my sexuality being known. Instead, I took my place behind my friend and grinded behind her as her hips and ass became possessed.

Always up for a challenge, I made sure that I kept up with her pace. She bent over and touched her toes all the while her ass cheeks clapped individually to the beat. I was in a trance. I wasn't sure what was happening, but the shit wasn't normal. I was seriously turned on and lusting after my best friend. I played it cool as we danced to another ten or so songs. By then her dogs were barking and I was out of breath and ready to call it a night.

On our way out of the club I felt as if we were being watched. Curious, I glanced around until my eyes connected with none other than Jacoby. He smiled at me and in return I gave him the bird. I then picked Meelah up bridal style to spare what feet she had left. I drove her car to McDonalds and then back to her house. By the time we reached her room we were both winded...mostly me from carrying her heavy ass halfway. We scarfed our food down and then reminisced about the fun night we'd just had.

Looking at Meelah, I saw her differently from the other times we'd been around one another. She was just so perfectly beautiful to me that night. She was always beautiful to me, but something was different tonight. As she continued to talk, I tuned her out and internally tried to understand my conflicted feelings. Before I could stop myself, I swept a few stray strands of hair from in front of her face. My hand then rested on her cheek as I leaned forward to kiss her.

She froze for a moment, but then I felt her body relax as she accepted my Big Mac flavored tongue. She herself tasted like chicken selects, but I couldn't have cared less. Glancing down I could see her chocolatey nipples hardening under the thin material of her dress. Instinctively, I reached for the one closest to me and gently squeezed as she moaned into my mouth. I grew uncomfortable as my man meat strained against the fabric of my black slacks. Reaching down to adjust my erection, Meelah abruptly pushed me away.

I stared at her trying to read her as she looked down into her own lap.

"Why'd you stop Lah Lah? Are you afraid of me?" I asked using reverse psychology.

"Ne-gro Puh-lease!!! Look around this bitch! I'm not afraid of shit!!!" Meelah shrugged, but I could see her trembling.

I gently grabbed her chin and pressed my lips onto hers. I slowly inched my way on top of her as I laid her back onto the bed. We were kissing sloppily and greedily. She was moaning into my mouth as I parted her legs with my knees. My left hand pulled her panties to one side and began to play with her pearl. I kissed and sucked on her neck knowing that I'd be leaving evidence of our passion behind. I pulled her dress over her head and tossed it onto the floor beside us.

She was clad only in a black lace matching thong and bra set. Her bra unclasped from the front and I wasted no time freeing her succulent C cups. I was pleasantly surprised when her breasts remained in place instead of falling sideways into her armpits. She was a work of art and I was happy that I was able to view her exhibit. Although I'd just eaten, I was starving for some chocolate so I pressed her tits together and did my best to shove them both into my mouth.

She howled as my long tongue went to work showing both of her breasts equal amounts of attention. I eventually snaked my tongue down her abdomen until I reached my destination. I had never eaten Nami's pussy before, so this was all new territory. For some reason, tonight I was craving Meelah's juicy box. As soon as my tongue grazed her swollen clit, her thick thighs instantly clamped down around my head making it impossible for me to escape if I wanted to...however, I didn't.

I felt her gripping at her sheets before her hands landed on the back of my head. She was bucking and humping my face as if her life depended on it. She was fresh and tasted so sweet. Meelah came four times before I showed her any mercy. When I finally came up for air, her essence was smeared all over my face and surprisingly, I didn't mind. It wasn't until I went to remove my pants that I realized that I had lost my promising erection.

Meelah being the dope friend that she is must have noticed the distressed look on my face and decided to come to my rescue.

She freed my willy and hastily placed him into her dewy mouth. I closed my eyes as I had done hundreds of times before and imagined that Meelah was Corey. Slowly I felt my blood start to pool into my center. As I became aroused, my dick grew inside of Meelah's mouth and even she appeared surprised once I reached my maximum expansion.

My full erection had grown over the years and now reached an impressive nine inches when I was fully aroused. Not bad for a little guy like myself. Meelah expertly worked her mouth on my tool as I began to drive my dick further and further down her esophagus. I growled and admired her ability to keep up with my pace without gagging. Figuring her throat had been stabbed enough, I withdrew myself from her oral cavity and rolled her over onto her back.

I knew time was of the essence if there was any hope of maintaining my erection. I noticed that her feminine softness had caused my dick to slightly deflate, so I rubbed my wood on her slick nether lips. I closed my eyes tightly and imagined her pussy was Corey's asshole. Miraculously, I felt my little man rock up once more. Without looking at Meelah I knowingly sank my smooth third leg into her fleshy gash. We both grunted in pleasure as I touched the bottom of her inner core.

She was so tight and wet that I had to take a moment or two to compose myself. Subconsciously, I knew that it was Meelah that I was sexing, however, for the sake of maintaining my erection *she* was currently a *he*. I knew later I'd feel bad about what we were doing, but tonight I was just going with the flow. Meelah's sexy ankles were locked around my neck as I drilled into her ass. The acoustics coming from her puss was enough to make me unload in her within minutes of entering her.

"Fuck Junior! Oh God, I love you boy! Yessssss...baby fuck this pussy!!!" She belted loudly.

As soon as she finished cheering me on, I realized that I was now stroking her with a limp noodle. I wasn't sure what did my erection in, but I was certain it was not coming back anytime soon. Embarrassed, I leaned into Meelah and pecked her on her lips. I rolled from on top of her and spooned her from behind. We'd slept in the same bed many times, but never this way.

Winded I said, “I’m sorry Lah Lah, I must be extremely tired tonight.”

“No worries Junior, I am exhausted myself after those back to back orgasms. I was tapping out anyway.” She shrugged making me feel a little better about myself.

One thing I couldn’t stop thinking about as I drifted off to sleep was the fact that I was fruiter than a fucking fruit basket!

« Chapter 15 Calm Before The Storm »

I HAD JUST FINISHED putting in the orders for a party of eighteen that had just entered my section at work. While most of the waiters dreaded the big parties because of the workload and the mess, I welcomed them. Hell, they were usually the biggest tippers. I walked over to the cook's window so that I could verbally reiterate my customers' orders. They had a lot of special requests and I knew that our new cook, Dex was bound to screw something up.

See what those arrogant ass cooks failed to grasp was that their oversights and late orders often determined the size of our tips. Some were actually attuned and used that as leverage. If a cook didn't like you, it wasn't unusual to receive your customer's orders super late. I didn't play that shit. I stayed on their asses, especially when I had a big order. I always thoroughly inspected the food as well prior to serving it to my customers. I was great at what I did, but like any job, the burnout at times was very real.

Satisfied that Dex understood the special requests, I decided to take a five minute breather. I had been running around all day without as much as a bathroom break. My manager always distributed our customers by the order in which we received our last customer. There were four waiters on staff today and since I had received the last table of customers, I wouldn't receive any more customers until the other three waiters received customers in their section. It was a fair system and kept favoritism down to a minimum.

I washed my hands, grabbed a Styrofoam cup and filled it with some sweet tea. I walked to our drab breakroom and quickly found a chair. After sitting down, I realized that I needed this break more than I'd realized. Closing my eyes I thought about what my next moves were going to be. My parents, especially my pops was on me to figure out what I wanted to do with my life. I knew that I wanted to attend college, but I was still undecided as to what I wanted to major in. I had only applied at four different universities and I was accepted by them all.

My grades had always been excellent...so were my siblings. The thing is, I wanted to take six months to a year off just to enjoy life without the burdens of waking up to attend classes every day. My mom seemed to understand where I was coming from, however, my dad as usual had the final say. Mama promised to work on convincing him to cut me a little slack. Hell, I was better off than Aimee right now. She'd put them through so much worse and was adding another mouth to feed into the equation. She didn't even finish high school!

I wasn't particularly good at anything extraordinary, but I was gorgeous. I wasn't big in stature, but I'd often wondered if I could make a living as a model. I knew better than to mention any of that shit to my dad though. I knew that whatever I presented to him had to be more reliable than a potential modeling career. A male model wasn't a masculine profession. I knew mama would have my back, however, she didn't have the final say.

As I was about to stand up to get back out onto the floor, Jacoby waltzed his ass into the breakroom and grinned at me. I really hated the fact that we still worked together and that I had to see him almost every day. The fact of the matter was, I needed my job. I couldn't afford to just up and quit. My pops would really be a thorn in my ass then. Jacoby didn't ever start shit at work so I was wondering what the hell he wanted. I know he didn't want anyone knowing he was a brown eye chaser, so his unwelcomed presence put me at a loss.

"Hey sexy, you miss me yet?"

"Hell naw! I can't stomach the sight of you. Just leave me the fuck alone Jacoby." I sneered.

"Believe it or not, I actually do miss your little ass. It wasn't part of the plan, but I was really feeling you. You do realize that it was all business and nothing personal right?"

"Look, I have customers that I have to get back to. There is nothing that you can ever say or do to make us okay again. You played me and I wasted my virginity on your punk ass. Why don't you do us both a favor and just quit. You're pimping muthafuckas out so you should be able to afford it!" I snapped.

His dark piercing eyes lowered as he said, "Damn, your anger turns me on!"

With that he grabbed my dick and tried to kiss me. I immediately slapped fire to his right cheek.

Rage took over his face as I braced for his physical retaliation. Just when he was about to raise his fist, a fellow waitress came into the room and told me that my table of eighteen were asking for me. I silently thanked her and God for intervening as I quickly exited the room to tend to the party. I knew Jacoby was furious and would be coming for me sooner than later.

∞

"Junior! I need you to help me set up these tables over here!" Mama yelled from the back of the venue.

Today was Aimee's baby shower and being the true perfectionist that she was, mama was driving us all crazy with the preparations. Mama and Aimee had opted on pink, brown and white for the theme colors. We had pooled our money together as a family to rent the Demers Banquet Hall for four hours. Mama was a huge Pinterest fan and had researched some amazing decorating ideas.

There was a massive candy bar that was comprised of nothing but various candies all pink in color. The three-tiered cake was pink, white and brown in color too. It was adorable. Pink, white and brown balloons were tastefully scattered about the building. Although some of the food, mainly the desserts were catered in, mama had made the bulk of the delicious food. The presentation was everything.

The shower was coed which doubled the overall turnout of the shower. A lot of Aimee's old friends were in attendance along with mama's nurse and teacher friends. Dad even had his old military family there. Aimee glowed and I prayed that this moment lasted forever. Her smile finally reached her eyes again and I knew that baby Skyy was sent to her in order to save her life.

The shower was extremely interactive and kept the guests busy with games the entire time. Finally Aimee sat in her Queen chair and began to open my niece's presents. She wasn't even here yet, but her ass was spoiled already. I was trying to determine how we were going to transport all the gifts when I heard, "What the hell is she doing here?!"

Being the nosy individual that I am, I turned around to investigate. I did a double take when I noticed none other than the infamous bitch Geena with my little brother in tow. She appeared to be inebriated as she staggered towards the festivities. She stopped only when she reached the table in which my parents were seated. Both of them donned angry scowls on their faces. My mom's face in particular said it all.

My dad was however the first to speak.

"What the hell are you doing here, Geena?" He seethed.

"Well it seems as if Marlon's invitation to his niece's baby shower was lost. Not wanting him to miss out on this joyous moment, I decided to show up and show out!" She exclaimed loudly.

"Look Geena, of course Marlon can stay, but *you* have to leave. Please do not make a scene here at my daughter's baby shower." Mama pleaded.

"Oh fuck you and that entitled junkie bitch!" Geena screamed.

This caught the attention of everyone who wasn't already privy to the drama unfolding within the room. Aimee even got out of her chair and waddled over to where my parents now stood.

"Geena, I know you did not seriously crash my baby shower with this foolishness. Now before you cause anymore chaos, you need to leave now or I will be on the phone with the cops." Aimee fumed.

"I'm not going anywhere, fuck..." Before Geena could finish my dad rushed over to her. She, however, brandished a gun before he made it to her.

"What Merlon? What? What did you *think* that you were about to do?" She asked my dad aiming the gun at his chest.

She continued, "Why did you make me love you just to treat me this way? I sacrificed so much of myself for you. I've done and become things I never thought I would. Do you think that I waited all of these years just to become a baby mama to a married broke ass security officer?! But you know what? Through all the hell you have drug me through, I still love you so much. You've raised your kids, it's time for you to come home to me and Marlon."

"He's still a baby and needs you. I need you desperately. Please baby. Come home." Geena cried causing her black eyeliner to trail down her face.

"Geena, you are a Goddamn fool if you think I'd ever leave my family for you! I've owned up to my responsibilities and I have no issues with taking care of my son, however, you and I have no future together. I've made it clear over and over again."

Geena looked from my dad to my mom and finally to Marlon before she let out a loud menacing laugh. Although she wore a smile on her face, she looked anything but happy. When the laughter ceased, a few tears graced her cheeks. She squatted down and began to whisper something to Marlon. As he nodded his head, she kissed him on his cheek.

Irritated and over Geena's tiresome charades, my father walked towards her in an attempt to once again get her to leave. Just as he reached out to touch her shoulder, she quickly aimed the gun at his head this time.

Alarmed gasps could be heard throughout the venue. I kicked myself because we had managed to cover all of our bases when it came to this baby shower, however, we had overlooked the need to hire security. Who needed security at a fucking baby shower?!

My dad was the first person to speak. "Geena, let's not do this right here in front of my family. There are kids here. *Our* kid is here. He doesn't need to see this. Now it is me you want, we can do this shit in an hour. The party will be over by then. Please just not in front of my wife and children." He tried to reason.

Geena's eyes looked as if she was processing what it was, he was saying. She looked remorseful. Tears flowed effortlessly down her face and I almost sympathized with her. In the midst of all of the chaos, I couldn't help but think if my dad had kept his dick in his pants, none of this bullshit would be happening right now.

Seeing that he was having some kind of effect on her, he continued, "I am sorry for all of the pain that I've caused you. My selfishness and arrogance has hurt a lot of people. If I could turn back the hands of time I..."

"What the fuck do you mean, if you could turn back the hands of time you would???'" She interrupted him midsentence.

"So, you regret meeting me now? You regret having our son?!" You are the one who chased me. I was fine before I met your sorry ass. I didn't have any drama, no complications and no fucking kids! You came into my life. You chased me relentlessly before I gave into your advances. You never even told me about the wife and kids that you are trying to protect now. You are a liar and because of your lies, you must die!" She screamed.

"Geena you don't have to do this!" My dad yelled while protecting my mother and sister by standing in front of them.

At the same time, my dad looked at me and I knew that he was about to reach for the gun that he always kept in his waistband. That was my cue to distract Geena's crazy ass. I had to think fast. The only leverage I truly had was my little brother's love for me. I decided to use it to my advantage.

Looking at my little brother, I smiled at him and then called out to him.

"Hey Lon Lon! Come here bro!" I called out.

His eyes lit up and he took off in my direction before Geena could process what was transpiring. As she reached for his arm, my dad quickly reached for his Glock, but not before Geena regained her senses and fired a shot in my dad's direction. Mama quickly pushed my father out of the way and I screamed as I watched as a huge hole formed in the center of her chest. Her white dress quickly transformed into a crimson red.

My dad let out an animalistic scream as he closed his eyes and emptied his clip in her direction. Geena must've had nine lives! Although she was hit more than a few times, she was still alive and kicking. None of her wounds appeared to be life-threatening. I finally snapped out of my trance and took off for my mother. I removed my shirt and used it to apply pressure to her chest. She was losing a lot of blood. She was still conscious and her breathing was haggard. My tears spilled onto her forehead as I begged for her to stay with me.

I heard my sister crying from a distance which alarmed me even more than I already was. Tearing my eyes away from my mama, I was mortified to see Geena laying on her back with Marlon laying on her chest. That wasn't the horrible part. The horrific part was the fact that she had her gun pointed at the top of Lon Lon's head. He was too young and innocent to even realize that the one person he sought out for comfort and protection was the very person endangering his life.

Aimee yelled, "Someone please shoot that bitch! She's going to kill my little brother!!!"

As soon as Aimee finished crying for help, Geena chanted, "Oh God, oh God, oh God" over and over again before a loud POW echoed throughout the building.

The silence was deafening as everyone stood in stunned silence.

My heart was in my throat as I took in the surreal scene around me. My mama's eyes were closed as I continued applying pressure to her chest. My little brother appeared to be asleep on his mother's chest, however, the fact that his brain matter was splattered all over the floor let us know that he was eternally resting.

My dad roared, "Noooooooooooooooo!" Just as the police came rushing in.

I heard several of the guests pointing them towards an injured Geena. As they approached Geena, she was still holding her weapon. The cops didn't fully understand the scene around them and were a bit cautious of everyone.

"Drop your weapon ma'am." One cop commanded.

I wasn't sure if she'd heard him because she didn't even blink at the sound of his voice.

"Ma'am, I'm not going to tell you again...drop your fucking weapon!!!"

I always assumed that the cop's verbal aggression was a result of him realizing that she'd killed the little boy lying on her chest.

I suppose the bass in his voice snapped her back to reality because she glanced around at everyone as if seeing all of us for the first time. She once again smiled exposing her blood covered teeth.

She then looked my dad directly in his eyes and yelled, "Merlon, you've killed all of us. *You* did this. I'll see you in hell!!!"

She raised her gun at no one in particular and the three cops standing over her literally blew her face off. None of their bullets even came near my lifeless baby brother.

« Chapter 16 The Aftermath »

A WEEK AND A HALF had lapsed and my dad was a mess. Hell, we were all a hot ass mess. We held Lon Lon's funeral four days after his mother took his life. I begged my pops to allow us to bury him in his Superman costume that he loved so much. His curly hair was slicked back and his long lashes rested on his cheeks. Luckily, his hair was long enough to cover the bullet hole. My little brother was one of those things in life that you didn't know that you wanted until you got it. I loved his little bad ass so much.

Jonah remained stoic through it all, while Aimee was an emotional wreck. She cried so much that I feared she'd be too dehydrated to maintain her pregnancy. Her due date was around the corner and her elevated stress levels couldn't be healthy. The doctors had informed us that due to my mom's severe blood loss coupled with a prolonged lack of oxygen, she was officially declared brain dead. They weren't detecting any brain activity.

She relied on all sorts of machines to keep her "alive", but she was gone as far as they were concerned. My father was in denial and refused to allow the staff to remove her from life support. The fact that my mother had opted to be an organ donor further infuriated my dad. He didn't want to discuss any of those options with those 'vultures' as he put it.

We all prayed over mama. I hated seeing her like that. She was always so lively and productive. I hated seeing her just laying there day after day. As much as I hated to lose her, I hated watching her lie motionless even more. We all begged papa to discontinue all life-sustaining measures, however, it wasn't until my maternal grandmother had a heart to heart with my father that he finally agreed to comply with the doctor's recommendations.

It was a Friday evening that we all sat somberly around mama's bed as the doctors removed her life support. We all sobbed with grief as we listened to her heart monitor as it flatlined after a few moments. She was pronounced at 2008...or 8:08 PM for those of you who are unfamiliar with military time. Her hospital room along with the waiting room were overflowing with people who loved her and were mourning the loss of my mom. Many of those who were present were also at Aimee's baby shower.

As much as my dad wanted to object to the transplant agency extracting her organs, he had no choice. The process was time sensitive so we had to wrap up our goodbyes fairly quick. No matter how hard I tried to fight it, I couldn't help but resent my dad for all that he'd caused. In the words of a dying Geena, he was the cause of all of this. He created the perfect scenario for this tragedy to take place. I tearfully stormed out of the room and rushed past all of the people in the waiting area.

I had to get out of there. I wished that Meelah were here, but she had already missed so much work behind me and my family issues that she'd been given a final counseling at work. I didn't want her to lose her job. She worked as a Certified Nurses' Assistant (CNA) and loved it. As weird as it sounds, as I neared the elevator, I felt him. I knew that he was nearby and that he was watching me. My vision was too blurry from tears to single him out though.

Once stepping on the elevator, I pressed the letter G for the ground floor. As the doors were closing, I saw an all too familiar hand slide in between them preventing them from closing. I watched as Corey slowly walked onto the elevator with his eyes looking into mine. His eyes mirrored mine as they were red and puffy. Even through my grief, this touched my heart. I knew how kind my mama was to him and the love that he had for her as a result.

Without waiting for the elevator doors to fully close, he roughly grabbed me in his arms and embraced me in the tightest hug. Although it wasn't my intentions, I broke all the way down inside of that elevator. My knees buckled and he pinned me into the wall of the elevator to keep me from falling. I felt so vulnerable and so transparent with Corey. I felt as if he could feel all of my pain without any words being exchanged. He beckoned me to let it all out as I wailed like a newborn baby.

I had just lost the first lady that I'd ever loved and the one person who I knew loved me most of all. The pain in my heart was so intense that I thought I'd die from the pain. How was I supposed to go on living without her? I'd always felt that my dad didn't love me as much as he merely tolerated me. How would he and I coexist without her? After some time and many curious elevator riders later, I had managed to pull myself together enough to walk outside of the hospital.

"Wait right here for a second, Junior." He commanded.

I was too frazzled to do anything other than what was asked of me. I was in a daze. I absentmindedly stood there as he walked away towards the parking garage. Minutes later, I saw a blue BMW pull up to the curb beside me. The windows were tinted, so it wasn't until Corey got out of the car and gently guided me inside that I knew for sure that it was him. The little homely boy that I'd always had a crush on sure had come a long way.

We were both quiet as he slowly pulled away from the curb. Although my face was expressionless, tears continued running down my face. He stole concerned glances at me from time to time. At some point, I realized that my hand was interlocked with his. I didn't ask any questions pertaining to our destination. I didn't care where he took me, I just wanted to ride forever.

∞

The sun was blazing on my face as I struggled to pry my swollen eyes open. I finally managed to open them ever so slightly. As my eyes adjusted to the bright rays of the sun, memories from the day before flooded back to me. Overwhelming sadness took over my whole being at the permanency of my new reality.

The right side of my lower stomach was on fire and I held my breath as I willed myself to peek at it. I groaned and fell back onto the bed.

"Fuck!" I blurted out.

"Isn't it a beauty?" Corey commented referring to the large letter C that was forever engraved into the skin of my abdomen.

I said nothing.

"I made you breakfast." I heard his deep voice announce as he walked further into the room.

Looking around, I didn't recognize my surroundings. I took a moment to admire the amount of money and detail that was put into the bedroom. The comforter and sheets were made by none other than Versace. Nothing as exquisite had ever graced my chocolate skin before. An oversized tv clung to the wall ahead and was encircled by the highest quality surround sound systems. A huge aquarium was built into the wall to my left. It was breathtakingly beautiful. I marveled at the exotic fish that occupied the space.

My eyes then landed on the sexy voice that had announced they'd prepared breakfast for me. There stood Corey clad only in deep maroon silk pajama bottoms. His bare chest caused my mouth to water more than the smell of the food he held out in front of him on a tray. His perfectly sculpted abs were beckoning my tongue to trail every crevice of his lower torso. My eyes bulged out their sockets when a huge letter M came into view on his stomach.

After he placed the food in front of me, I looked up into his handsome face and saw nothing but sadness behind his eyes. He gave me a weak smile, but I saw right through it.

I decided to ignore our apparent matching tattoos for now.

"Where are we, Corey?" I asked.

"This is my crib. What do you mean?" He stated looking slightly offended.

"This is really nice man. For real. Where's my goddaughter? I know it's my weekend with her, but I'm so messed up right now."

"Man, Junior you're good. She's with her trifling ass mama right now. Focus on you. She is good."

"I appreciate all of this. I can't remember the last time I had something to eat." I stated shoving an entire slice of bacon into my mouth.

"It's nothing. You've been there and fed me when my stomach was empty. Loyalty is everything to me. I'll always have your back if you need anything." He vowed.

I simply nodded my head as I greedily scarfed my food down.

Aimee had reached out to me and told me that mama's funeral was scheduled in two days. She'd already found me a suit and said that Corey had paid for it already. I was still camped out at his house not ready to face the world. I promised her that I'd be home the next day so that I could face everyone and prepare for mama's services.

Corey had rarely left my side during the time I'd been at his house. He'd done everything in his power to cheer me up. He spoiled me by helping me bathe and feeding me when I felt too weak to do it myself. He never tried to have sex with me and I loved him that much more. He was very affectionate in the way he handled me. He kissed my tears away when the pain became more than I could bear. I could've stayed hidden away with him forever!

The day before my mother's funeral, I noticed that I had several missed calls and texts instructing me to call from my sister, brother, Meelah and pops. A feeling of dread came over me and I knew it couldn't be good, so I ignored everyone by turning off my phone. My heart couldn't take any more pain. I wanted to feel good and, in this moment, only Corey could accomplish that feat.

Corey and I were making out and wrestling in the living room when his doorbell began to ring incessantly. Initially, Corey tried to block out the persistent visitor, but he soon grew agitated and flung his heavy door open with an attitude. Being the nosy person that I am, I followed him to see what was going on. A beautiful caramel skinned girl who sported an annoyed expression on her face was standing in the doorway. Corey did not look pleased to see her at all.

"Man Charisma, what the hell are you doing here?! How do you even know where the fuck my crib is at?" Corey snapped.

"Nigga, if you would answer your muthafucking phone, I wouldn't have to just pop the fuck up. Why haven't I heard from you in almost a week, Corey?" The girl he called Charisma asked.

"Charisma don't come to my door asking me about my whereabouts! You ain't my woman. I don't owe you or no other bitch any explanations. Again, how did you find out where I live?"

"Corey you don't have to talk to me like this. I've missed you, that's all. It doesn't matter how I found out where you live. Can I come in baby? I've missed that big ass dick daddy." She purred.

I came from around the door making my presence known. Although I knew Corey wasn't my man and didn't even verbally acknowledge his attraction for me, I felt that he was mine. I got a better look at Charisma and realized she looked a lot like the actress Sanaa Lathan. Baby girl was bad! If I wasn't secure in my own flawless features, I would've been insecure as hell in her presence.

She looked genuinely surprised to see me. Her face was twisted up with confusion I'm sure because we were both dressed only in our boxers. I'm sure we were looking suspect, but I didn't care what she thought of my black ass. I wanted her to leave and I wanted to continue to be carefree with my boo.

"Ummmm, what's going on Corey? What is this?" She inquired looking me up and down before her eyes landed back on him.

"What the fuck you mean what is this? This is my homeboy. He's like family so watch your mouth. His family took me in when I had nowhere else to go. He needs me now, so he's going to be staying with me for a while." Corey replied nonchalantly.

"Oh, I'm sorry baby. Can I come in and make it up to you?" She pouted seductively.

I couldn't help but roll my eyes as he stepped back allowing her entry into my new safe haven. My eyes bore holes into the both of them as he threw her over his shoulder and beelined it to his bedroom. Moans were soon heard coming from his room. With each bang of his headboard into the wall, my heart fractured in another place. How could he do this to me again?

I grabbed my phone off of the coffee table and powered it on. I ordered an Uber and noted that my driver was approximately four minutes away. I quickly threw on the clothes that I'd worn over to his house, took one last look around and walked out of the front door just as Corey growled that he was cumming. I fucking hated his ass.

« Chapter 17 Dear Junior »

MY THOUGHTS AND emotions were all over the place on the ride back home. Losing my mama and my little brother within weeks of one another and then to have my heart ripped open by the love of my life, yet again was just too much. I didn't realize that I was crying until my Uber driver, Jean asked me if I were okay. I lied and assured him that I was and looked out of the window for the remainder of the ride.

Once reaching my destination, I tipped and thanked Jean for the safe ride. I got out and jogged up to my front door. I removed my key from my pants pocket and inserted it into the keyhole. I twisted the doorknob and was surprised that the door didn't budge. I repeated that same song and dance without luck.

"What the fuck?!" I mumbled under my breath.

Growing increasingly annoyed, I began to ring the doorbell with a vengeance. All I wanted was my bed and a little peace. After what seemed like hours, I heard what sounded like paper coming from underneath the door. I looked down and noticed an envelope with my name written on it in my father's handwriting.

Taking a deep breath, I pinched my nose to contain my growing anger. Why the fuck was my dad sliding me letters under the door, playing and shit. Why wasn't my key working and why wouldn't he just let me the fuck in!

Squatting down, I picked up the envelop. I impatiently ripped it open and read the letter's contents.

Junior,

I hate to even refer to you as such. You have brought me and this family great shame. I've always told your mama that you were soft and I knew deep inside that you were going to end up being a fag. As far as I'm concerned, you are no longer my son. You are as dead to me as Marlon is. I didn't raise you to be a punk, but your mama allowed your marshmallowy ass to prance around acting like a little girl. Maybe that's the problem...you kids had too much growing up. First your sister disgraced us and then you and this gay shit. Just in case you're wondering what this is about...check out the video that I sent to you.

Just then I remembered all of the calls and texts I'd been receiving from everyone. Pulling my phone out, I scrolled down to my dad's name and without even clicking on the video, I knew that Jacoby had done the unimaginable. He had actually sent that disgraceful video to the people I loved. I backed out of my dad's name and began to skim over some of the other texts I'd received from my sister, brother and Meelah. While my sister and Meelah expressed sympathy and compassion for my current situation, Jonah was clearly disgusted.

He called me every derogatory name in the book and essentially told me that I was dead to him as well. That statement brought my attention back to my dad's letter.

How could you as a man allow another man to bend you over and fuck you son? The very thought of it repulses me to my very core. You are my biggest regret to date. I hate that you carry my name. Jonah should've held that honor as he is more deserving. Your key didn't work because I changed all of the locks. You are no longer welcome in my home.

I've also confiscated your car from the hospital. Since it is in my name, I have given it to Jonah. Since you like to ride dicks so much, you can have those muthafuckas take you to your destinations! After today, do not step foot onto my yard because I will have you arrested for trespassing. If you should see me out in the streets, act like you do not know me.

Lastly, your mother's funeral...is off limits to you. You better not let me catch your faggoty ass around my wife fucking up her legacy. Do yourself and the world a favor and try not to catch AIDS.

Take care.

Merlon Sr

At the conclusion of my letter, I was a hysterical mess. I had lost pretty much everyone and everything. I had never felt so alone in my life. I needed mama more than I ever had before. I slid down onto the ground using the door. I cried like a baby as I mourned all that I had lost in the last couple of weeks. How could he be so cold as to prevent me from attending my own mama's funeral? At first, I defiantly told myself that I would go despite what he had to say about it, but I thought better of it. I didn't want to cause any chaos at her funeral.

Truthfully, I was too ashamed to face everyone anyway. I didn't know how far Jacoby's reach was, however, I couldn't help but to assume that everyone had seen it. Thoughts of wanting to die consumed me. My dad had the audacity to say that I was his biggest regret?! I would've surely assumed that meeting Geena would've been his biggest regret. Suddenly, I felt myself being pulled up to my feet. I assumed that it was my dad coming to whoop my ass for lingering around on his porch.

Peering up, I realized that it was Jean, my Uber driver.

"Pardon me, but I stuck around to make sure that you got inside safely because you looked as if you were having the day from hell. I couldn't help but notice that you are in a bit of a crisis man. I'm not sure what demons you're facing here, but I can take you somewhere else if you like...for free of course."

For a lack of any other choices, I nodded and followed the kind man back to his vehicle. I didn't know where to go. I didn't want to be a burden to anyone. Plus, as I said before, I was too humiliated to face anyone right now. I just wanted to crawl into a crevice and disappear. I sat in the front seat beside Jean as he continued working, transporting passenger after passenger. By the time midnight rolled around, I still hadn't scrounged up any places that I could go.

Jean must've caught on to that because we eventually ended up at what he announced as his house. It was pretty small, but it was immaculate. Nothing was out of place. Jean gave me a brief tour of his home and told me that I could crash on his couch for as long as I needed to. He gave me an oversized t-shirt and some shorts to sleep in and whipped up what he referred to as his famous Ramen noodles.

He told me that he wasn't much of a cook and ate out most of the time due to his sporadic schedule. That much was evident as he was on the bear side, but not necessarily in a bad way. He wasn't really my type, but for those into bearded bears, I suppose he was a catch. He attributed his midnight black skin to his Jamaican roots. He was born in Texas, however, both of his parents immigrated to the U.S a few years before he was born. He was seemingly straight, single and did not have any kids.

Jean was twenty-seven and had been working as an Uber driver for eight months. He claimed the money was nice and the flexible schedule was even better. He also did DoorDash as well. He seemed like an overall great guy. He was kind enough to take me in when I wasn't ready to face the world just yet. I told him pieces of my story. Most of the scabs were just too fresh to snatch off right now. I did tell him that I was gay and that my family didn't agree with it. The details were insignificant.

Thankfully, my homosexual disclosure didn't seem to make him uncomfortable like most macho men. For the life of me, I will never understand why people assumed that just because you're gay, you're automatically attracted to every species of the same sex. Just because someone is gay, does NOT make them desperate. If anything, most of the gay people I'd encountered were extremely selective when it came to selecting their counterparts. I wished people would stop flattering themselves.

The feelings that swept over me on the day of my mother's funeral were indescribable. My chest hurt so badly that I thought I was having a heart attack. Jean tried everything in his power to get me to go, but I didn't want to cause a scene so we waited outside of the church to see as much as we could. I had even managed to swipe an obituary from one of her fellow nurses. We trailed behind the funeral procession until we arrived at mama's final resting place.

There had to be over a thousand people there to bid mama farewell. She was certainly loved by a lot of people. I was too far to hear what was being said. but her casket was beautiful from a distance. The infamous white doves were released signifying every year God allowed her to bless us with her presence. My family all looked devastated. My nana had to be restrained several times because she kept attempting to open the casket to climb in. I begged Jean to pull off before she was lowered into the ground.

There was no way that I could survive after witnessing her being lowered into the ground. How did people survive after enduring grief like this? It would be one thing to lose her to natural causes, but to be murdered was an entirely different matter. She didn't deserve any of that and neither did Marlon. I wanted to dig his funky ass mama up and kill her ass again. I later found out that Mama was buried next to Marlon. I wasn't sure how I felt about it, but what could I do about it? I had no rights or say in the matter.

« Chapter 18 Overrated »

I HADN'T CALLED OR returned to my job at IHOP, so I knew I was fired. When I wasn't sulking and feeling sorry for myself, I made food deliveries with Jean to appease him. He initially tried to share his earnings with me, but I'd always decline. He was going out of his way enough on my behalf and I felt like such a burden. The only people that I truly missed were Aimee and Meelah. They both called and texted a lot throughout the day, but I was at a loss as to what to say to them. So I opted to say nothing.

Christmas rolled around and Jean had purchased a tree that I affectionately referred to as a Charlie Brown tree. That was the skeetest Christmas tree I'd ever seen before, but somehow it put a smile on my face every time I glanced at it. I didn't have any money to purchase my friend anything, so I took the liberty of rearranging his bedroom the way I heard him say he wanted it. I had also managed to buy a Christmas card from our corner drug store.

I couldn't wait until he came home and saw what I'd done to his bedroom. I cooked some chicken in the air fryer along with rice pilaf and broccoli. It wasn't much to some, but it was everything to me. I always went out of my way to cook and clean his already clean apartment so that I wouldn't wear out my welcome as fast.

Around eight in the evening, I heard his keys jingling outside of the front door. A smile took over my face as his face came into view. He was holding a small bag in his hand. As he approached me, he handed the bag to me.

"What's this?" I inquired.

"Look and see with your impatient ass." He joked, but was telling the truth.

I squealed with excitement because I truly was not expecting anything for the first time ever on Christmas.

"It sure smells good in here Junior."

"Oh, that must be some of the cologne I borrowed from you." I gushed.

Shaking his head, he replied, "No, I smell some bomb ass food."

Embarrassment washed over me as I realized my error. I quickly ran down what I'd cooked for dinner. I then redirected my attention to my gift.

Looking into the bag, I saw what appeared to be a card. I hurriedly picked up the card and carefully ripped it open. Pulling out its contents, I read the card first. Tears welled in my eyes at the thoughtfulness of this guy I'd just met. My eyes then shifted to my actual gift.

"See, I pay attention to more than people realize. I heard you mention before that you'd always wanted to see the Tran Siberian Orchestra perform…well I got us front row seats."

"Oh my God!!! Thank you soooooo much Jean! This is one of the best gifts I've ever received!" I shouted jumping up and down.

I would've hugged him if it wasn't for me not wanting to make him uncomfortable. Sexuality was such a grey area and I tried never to cross that line with people. That's how many people got killed.

"You seriously didn't have to do any of this. You've done so much for me already. I don't think I'll ever be able to repay you for your selflessness and kindness." I stated getting choked up.

"Ahhh don't mention it. I'm happy to do it. Your reaction was well worth the price of those tickets."

"Follow me, I want to show you something." I instructed.

I led the way to his room and handed him the card before opening his bedroom door.

"Read it after you see your gift."

He nodded his head.

"Are you ready?" I asked in a teasing manner.

"Junior, if you don't open that damn door already!" He chuckled.

"Alright, alright! Now, who's being impatient?" I asked pushing the door open.

I flicked on the light and turned my attention to his face hoping he liked the way I had rearranged everything. Although his place was small, his bedroom was fairly big. It took me the better part of the day to pull everything off.

His face was stoic and then I noticed his jaw twitching. I had imagined many expressions crossing Jean's face, however, this was not one of them. He then looked overwhelmed as he slowly walked about the room. I watched as his fingers trailed his dresser and the pictures on them. With his back facing me, he focused on positioning all of the items on his dresser within a certain distance from one another. It was odd watching him obsess with getting everything just right.

After standing in the doorway for approximately ten minutes witnessing his odd behavior, I cleared my throat. He froze before slowly turning around to face me. Embarrassment washed over his face. I truly believe that in his trance, he'd forgotten I was even in his presence.

Looking at his feet he mumbled, "I guess you're going to leave now aren't you? You know my secret. I have obsessive compulsive disorder. I truly do appreciate the thought and effort, but I hate when people touch my stuff. Now the equilibrium in here is off. That's why I never changed the room around myself."

"I'm not going to leave unless you want me to Jean. I think it looks great in here. It's much roomier. You have access to more of your room. Please leave it this way." I pouted.

Cracking his first smile since we'd entered his room, he walked over to me and sucked on my bottom lip. His actions surprised me because I'd never gotten gay vibes from him before. My body responded to him immediately. I was sexually frustrated and ready to pounce on just about anything. I knew we shouldn't cross that line for several reasons, but in that moment, I wanted to be loved...physically.

I hadn't physically been touched since I left Corey's house. That is a long time with no physical human contact. I hungrily suckled on his tongue as I grabbed a hold of his meat. Jamaican men had third legs like no other! I could barely wrap my hand around the entire circumference of his man meat.

Resting his head into thc crook of my neck, Jean stated, "You do smell good as fuck. Even better than the food you prepared."

I simply responded with a moan.

With my first sexual experience being such a negative one, I prayed that Jean showed me why the world was so sex crazed. I wanted him to prove to me that sex wasn't overrated.

Looking into my eyes Jean said, "I don't know what you're doing to me Junior. I have never even considered being with a man before, yet being around you, it is all that I can think about anymore. I can't lie to myself any longer. You make me happy and I love having you here with me."

With that, he pushed me onto the bed. I lifted my hips to allow him to remove my briefs. I snatched my shirt off and stroked my dick in anticipation of what was to come.

Jean did a slow seductive striptease for me with his eyes lowered. While he didn't possess the toned, washboard abdomen that I was used to, he was my Blair Underwood tonight. Once he was completely nude, I leaned back and stared at his body.

I grew worried as I wondered how I was going to fit his horse-sized cock into my backside. Fear consumed me, but I refused to back down now. I was super horny and wanted Jean to make love to me in the worst way.

As precum oozed from the tip of his erection, I took my index finger to swipe up the spillage so that I could sample his nectar. My actions seemed to increase his arousal as he bit his bottom lip. My eyes never left his as he ordered me to turn over onto my stomach.

I heard him walk over towards his dresser and retrieve something.

"Get up on your knees and arch your back." He commanded.

I followed his orders and made an arch deep enough to rival the McDonalds arch.

"Relax Junior." He directed.

I felt something warm and slippery being applied to my rectum. It felt great.

Jean then took his right index finger and slowly worked it inside of me. My body tensed up, not really from pain, but more from surprise. I still wasn't used to anything being inside of my asshole.

"Take a deep breath and relax like I told you to."

I did.

As Jean slowly and carefully worked his finger in and out of me, I felt my body start to relax as his finger fucked my backdoor. Once he was satisfied that I was sufficiently taking one finger, he inserted another one. He repeated the same process until I once again relaxed. I was backing my ass up onto his fingers in anticipation.

Once he removed them, I loudly cried out as I felt his tongue as it cycloned around my brown eye. I stopped breathing for a full two minutes when the tip of his pointed tongue initially grazed against me. I thought I was going into respiratory distress in that muthafucka!!! Never had I felt anything so tantalizingly incredible. As I called to our Father in heaven, I knew then that sex certainly wasn't overrated. No one had ever eaten my groceries before, but I now knew that it would forever be a staple in my relationships.

I immediately felt a sense of loss when he withdrew his tongue from within me. However, he did not leave me hanging for long. I heard him open up a condom and apply it to his sex organ. I shuddered when the head of his penis tapped on my asshole. He slowly pushed my rectal walls aside while loudly groaning. I glanced back at him and his eyes were closed while his mouth formed a perfect O.

It was a little uncomfortable, but nothing compared to the first disastrous encounter. He talked me through the process and it helped me tremendously. While Jean had never been with a man sexually before, he had screwed several women in their asses in the past. My biggest concern was the nagging feeling of having to fart and shit. By trying to prevent any solids and gases from slipping out, it made it slightly difficult to relax.

Jean's balls were loudly slapping up against my own from behind. The acoustics in his room were marvelous. Jean told me that he had only inserted a few inches of himself inside of me, which I was grateful for. He continued to deliver slow and deliberate strokes until his body convulsed as he collapsed on top of my sore body. Jean wasn't really my type, but his D game was certainly on point! A guy could get used to this.

« Chapter 19 Black And Blue »

IT'S AMAZING WHAT ONE can learn from watching every day people's Youtube channels. It took lots of practice, but I was now an expert at hiding the black eyes and bruises. Jean was Lucifer in disguise. It turns out that not only did he suffer from OCD, but he was also bipolar. At least that's what he told me in an attempt to get me to stay.

If he came home and things were not exactly how he felt they should be, he'd initiate an argument which almost always led to a physical altercation. My parents had always raised me to fear no man, and I cannot say that I was scared of him, but what I feared was being alone. I still had not reached out to my sister or to Meelah, which I hated myself for. My niece whom I couldn't wait to meet had to be around five months now and I had yet to meet her.

If it weren't for social media, I wouldn't even know what she looked like. She looked a lot like me and Aimee...as well as mama. I never thought it was possible to love someone I'd never met as much as I loved my little niecey pooh. I also kept tabs on Shateara through Corey's social media pages. Something needed to give. I knew I had to get away from Jean's nutty ass. The fights were getting super old. Trust me, I fought his ass back every time, but I was no match for his psychotic strength. Those crazy muthafuckas bench press cars for sport!

As with virtually all abusers, Jean would express remorse and promise that he'd never hit me again. He'd buy me shit and be on his best behavior for a day or two only to snap and whoop my ass again. My body was covered in bruises in varying stages of the healing process.

I still wasn't working nor was I in school, therefore, I didn't leave the house often. I think Jean preferred it like that. He didn't like when I ventured off too far. I guess he knew if I did, I just might not return. I needed to find a job as soon as possible so that I could devise my escape plan. I couldn't simply just leave now because I had nowhere to go. I didn't want to impose on Meelah and her family. I had to find my own way.

I had been going on secret interviews for weeks, but so far nothing had materialized. It was exhausting because no one wanted to take a chance on someone as inexperienced as I was. The only job that I'd ever had was at IHOP and I didn't want to put them down as a reference because in the end I was practically a no call no show.

Through it all, my faith never wavered. I knew that God had better plans for me. I viewed my experiences as stepping stones that led to greater days.

"Damn, he really fucked me up this time!" I exclaimed under my breath.

I did my best to cover up the bruising and swelling in my face, while also trying to conceal that I was wearing makeup at all. Content with the results, I headed towards the front door.

"Where the fuck you think you going?" Jean barked.

"My friend Meelah wanted to meet up today...remember? I haven't seen her since my mama's funeral." I stated regrettably.

"Man fuck both of those bitches! As far as I'm concerned, they are both dead to us. How are you making plans to chill when I don't smell shit cooking?!"

"I made a roast earlier...what do you mean?"

He got up and stormed over to the stove. Opening up the lid

that contained the roast, his face grew tight.

"Nigga, I told your sweet pickle ass that I don't eat red meat no more!!! I go out and slave for us all day, every day while you lie on your lazy ass cooking me bullshit that I can't eat!" Jean yelled with disgust.

He lifted his right hand and smacked the pan across the room. Roast, vegetables and gravy flew everywhere! I'm not exactly sure what it was that struck a nerve, but seeing the food I'd spent hours preparing splattered all over the previously clean kitchen caused me to snap!

I caught Jean off guard as I charged at him with another pan in my hand. Before he could react, I clocked him upside his head. Although in a daze, he quickly recovered and wrestled the pan from me. This didn't deter me. I was sick of him bullying and whooping my ass every day. If his ass wanted to fight, I wouldn't let him down. I punched him in his head with all my might. I was getting the best of him this day, although I'm sure the Ambien I slipped into his Budweiser helped a little.

At some point during our brawl, he clothes lined me and I fell onto my back. He wasted no time in pouncing on me. He wrapped his large hands around my neck and began to squeeze. I instantly panicked because I had never been deprived of oxygen for so long. I clawed at his hands trying to inflict enough pain that he'd release me. I felt my life slipping away and couldn't help but to be embarrassed by my senseless ending.

I wished my death were a more dignified one. Instead I was being choked out on a kitchen floor covered in roast juice. I ran out of fight and my arms finally retreated to my sides. The pain in my lungs was inconceivable. Just as the final page of my life was about to turn, I heard a feminine growl somewhere in the distance. Soon my lungs were able to receive oxygen again. I breathed heavily as I turned over onto my side in an attempt to fill my lungs to capacity.

I'm not exactly sure how much time had lapsed before I was able to assess my surroundings. My eyes first landed on an unconscious and bloodied Jean. His head and face was all lumped up. I checked him and unfortunately…yet fortunately he was still breathing. Shit, I was too pretty for prison!

"What the hell…" I mumbled.

"Junior! Oh my God Junior! I thought that son of a bitch had killed you! You weren't moving and I was so scared." Meelah shrieked running over to me.

After hugging and kissing me for several moments, she pulled away and started assessing me for injuries. I assured her that I was fine, but not before she peeped the various wounds he'd afflicted upon me in the past. Although her eyes spoke thousands of words, her mouth never opened to speak and I appreciated her for that.

"We have to get out of here before that asshole wakes up. I'm not sure he can handle these hands again." Meelah joked.

I simply nodded and accepted her assistance to get to my feet.

I glanced around the unhappy place I had called home for what I knew would be the last time. I then walked over to Jean who was lying spread eagle in the supine position and kicked his ass as hard as my leg allowed me to in his nuts. He was still out of it, but his non-verbals gave me all the entail that I needed. He was in excruciating pain.

Being the nasty little bastard that I was, I reached from the lowest depths of my esophagus and hacked up the thickest loogie of my life. I allowed my blood tinged saliva to accumulate in my mouth for a couple of minutes. I then nastily painted his battered face with my chunky mouth juices. Satisfied, I set off to pack what little belongings that I had before he roused. If I'd learned anything from being with Jean, it would have to be never to allow another man to put his hands on me. I'd kill them first...

« Chapter 20 C.N.A. »

I WAS IN DESPERATE NEED of a gig and I was in no position to be picky. I was living on Meelah's couch and was sick of relying on the bus to get me to my destinations. Meelah told me about a job fair being held at her place of employment. As I mentioned before, she worked at a nursing home and told me that if hired, they would do on the job training and certify me there as a Certified Nurse's Assistant. Now I know that I just told you all that I was in no position to be picky, but damn! I wasn't trying to fuck around with those old people like that.

The only other time I had ever been to a nursing home was when I accompanied Meelah to visit her grandmother and that place stunk to high heaven! The vivid stench of hot piss and shit was eternally etched in my nostrils. My journey down memory lane caused me to immediately turn Meelah's offer down several times, however, I eventually agreed to go. Hell, what did I have to lose? I had already lost it all.

The job fair was held on a Friday and my initial thoughts about the facility were vastly different from the facility my friend's grandmother resided in. This place was immaculate and no offensive odors were detected during our tour of the building. The staff was extremely friendly and welcoming. Two other people who were also friends with Meelah, came to the fair with me. Me and a girl named Harmony were hired on the spot. The other girl, Dawn was turned down for two reasons. The first being that she did not pass the drug screening process and secondly because she didn't have a high school diploma.

Well, she claimed that she had one, but that is neither here nor there. All I know is that I have never seen her black ass again after that day. Meelah had already given me a heads up, so I had my clean piss sample safely tucked under my nuts. I passed with flying colors…so to speak. Me and Harmony twerked our juicy asses out in the parking lot to celebrate. I was offered eleven dollars an hour to work overnights with the promise of twelve dollars after completing my CNA training. I couldn't believe my good fortune. I had never made that much money before in my life. Before we even left the parking lot, I had already calculated how many paychecks it was going to take in order to get my own place and vehicle.

My mama always told me to never count my chickens before they hatched, but those bitches were counted honey! I was scheduled to start general orientation that upcoming Monday. My new career filled me with anxiety because it was so vastly different from my last job. Meelah knew that I was trying to get the bag and assured me that they had as much overtime that I could physically stand. That was music to my ears. With the little bit of money that I had, I went and treated myself to a much needed mani and pedi. I couldn't start my new job looking destitute and shit…although I really was. Meelah tried to pay, but she had already done more than enough for me.

Monday morning rolled around fast! I kicked myself for drinking the night before because my head was now pounding. My general orientation was boring and pretty basic. Harmony and I sat in the back and clowned around to keep ourselves awake. I really didn't know her outside of the handful of times Meelah had brought her around, but she seemed cool enough. She was a cute brown skin girl. She kind of reminded me of the actress Malinda Williams…only she was a BBW.

I was grateful that the facility treated us to breakfast and lunch because I had spent my last few coins at the nail salon. I didn't have any money for food. I know my priorities appeared to be fucked up, but I'd rather go hungry than to have these heifers seeing me looking rough. I was thankful that Harmony had rejected my offer to give her gas money for bringing me to work. Truthfully, I didn't have any to give.

More than anything, it would have made for an awkward situation. I think Harmony just enjoyed the company during our forty minute commute. We had so many "special" guest speakers that I couldn't even begin to match their names with their job titles. They all pretty much looked the same too. I did, however, remember the Human Resource chick. She was essentially the most valuable person to grace my presence all day.

By the end of the day, we were given our schedules, assigned permanent divisions, given our name badges and two sets of scrubs to get started. Looking at my name badge, I felt a sense of pride. I finally felt some sense of purpose and belonging. I wasn't entirely sure what being a Nurse's Assistant entailed, but at any rate, I was pretty stoked about my new job.

There was a lot of unfamiliar medical jargon being thrown around and I couldn't wait to be able to throw those fancy words around myself one day. The woman hosting our general orientation gave us a checklist of tasks that we needed to complete by a certain time frame and that's when shit begin to get real.

I didn't know what half of the shit was and the other half was shit I was pretty sure I didn't want to do. I loved old people and all, but the exact quantity of my love for them was in question as I reviewed the checklist. I prayed to Jesus and asked for strength. I couldn't quit because I had already given IHOP my ass to kiss. I needed the Ben Franks and I needed them yesterday!

The next evening, I reported to work thirty minutes early thanks to Harmony. I was almost always late for everything, yet being on another person's time, I had to be ready when they told me to be ready. I reported to my assigned division and stood at the nurse's station. Since I still had approximately ten minutes or so to kill, I studied my surroundings. Everyone appeared to be preoccupied by the typical change of shift banter. I glanced at the assignment sheet that was discussed during our general orientation. I saw that I was orienting with a CNA named Shaneice.

The CNAs were to wear all navy blue scrubs while the nurses wore all white scrubs. That policy was nice as it helped me differentiate between the two. Armed with the information that I knew, I set my eyes on the females wearing all blue. I asked two people if they were Shaniece and they told me no. No one had seen her yet.

For a lack of other choices, I decided to wait a few more minutes for her to stroll her tardy ass in. Not too long after, I saw this horse face chick hobbling her big ass down the hall. Nonetheless, I prayed that she was Shaniece because I was anxious to get started. As she got closer to the nurse's station, I saw that her name tag did indeed read SHANIECE in big bold letters.

Instead of hounding her like a groupie, I allowed her unpunctual ass enough time to set her bags down and get situated before approaching her. A few moments after she secured her bags in her locker, she came up to the desk and reviewed the assignment sheet. She instantly became upset.

Glaring at one of the elderly white nurses behind the desk, she interrupted their report and barked, "Vicky! Why was I pulled from my usual assignment?! You know that I don't get pulled because I have the most seniority! Also, can someone else 'orientate' this Junior person? I don't feel like it tonight. I'm already running behind and he will just slow me down!"

The nurse that she had referred to as Vicky blinked a few times prior to glancing at her 14k gold Bulgari watch. She then looked back up at Shaniece and said, "Shaniece, please don't ever interrupt me while I am in the middle of report again for something this trivial. You were pulled because you are nearly thirty minutes late. You will train the new orientee because the Director of Education assigned that task for you to do due to the seniority that you were so quick to mention you had a moment ago. Now if you have a problem with any of the things we've just discussed, you are welcome to clock out and go home. Then you can take it up with nursing administration in the morning."

I could tell Shaniece was furious, but she did not challenge Nurse Vicky any further. I didn't miss the wink that Nurse Vicky shot my way and I instantly took a liking to her. She was certainly no pushover. Shaniece simply wobbled off down our assigned hall with me quietly trailing behind her.

It was the longest night ever because Shaniece rarely spoke to me at all. She only asked for me to assist her in repositioning two residents and that was essentially the extent of our dialogue for the night. I was overjoyed when seven rolled around and it was time to clock out. Although my first night on the job sucked, I was happy that Harmony's went a little better than my own.

∞

A week later...

I was scheduled off the night before because I had to attend my weekly CNA training during the day on Thursday. The class was extremely interactive. It was half lecture and half hands on skills. I really enjoyed the class portion and felt I learned a lot. We were covering the process of giving a resident a shower. It didn't sound too complex. I had been washing my own ass for nineteen years, so how difficult could it be? I was slightly taken aback by how systematic the process was and by how many wash cloths were used to bathe one person.

After the lecture part of our class concluded, we took a lunch break. Thankfully, this company believed in feeding the employees every day for free, so I found my place at the back of the long line. My stomach growled the closer I got to the front of the line. Harmony was outside smoking. She had brought a sandwich for lunch, so we decided to meet back inside of the classroom. Carrying my cheeseburger and fries, I was the first person to get back into the room. Glancing around, I noticed that the majority of my fellow trainees had left their purses behind.

I hated to act on what I was thinking, but I really needed some money. I hadn't eaten much the day before because I didn't have any money and it was a long time before pay day. All Meelah typically had at home was Ramen Noodles and I couldn't stomach those anymore. Her mom would sell any food with a value higher than that. Again, I knew if I had asked Meelah for a loan until payday she would've gladly given it, but I already felt like a huge burden.

I randomly grabbed the purse closest to me and quickly raided it. Nothing! Placing the purse how I had found it, I grabbed the purse next to it and found six crisp Ben Franks folded neatly inside of the matching Michael Kors wallet. This purse belonged to a young African girl named Imani. I stared at the small stack and fought with myself.

I literally had two little people from opposing sides bickering over my shoulders. One was good, while the other was not. That money could have been for Imani's rent or her children. On the other hand, I had over two weeks until I would see my first paycheck. I knew my mama was turning over in her grave at how low I was willing to stoop in order to survive.

"God and mama up in heaven, please forgive me for what I'm about to do." I prayed a loud as I peeled off one of the bills before returning the rest of the money into Imani's wallet.

I reasoned that what I had done wasn't too bad since I had only taken one hundred dollars. Hell, I could've taken all of her fucking money! The average person would have without a second thought. I internally promised to repay her somehow. As soon as I took a seat and bit into my burger, Harmony walked into the room.

"Junior, I can't believe you are eating that shit. Is it good? You know that's the same bullshit they feed the residents, right? Meelah says they put shit in the food to make the old people gain weight. All of the workers who eat the food here, end up fat as hell." She said matter-of-factly.

I couldn't help but to smirk as I envisioned Shaniece's Rasputia looking ass. Baby girl definitely wasn't missing any meals or snacks!

"It tastes alright, I guess. But anyway, I can use a little extra thickness hoe!" I joked as I scarfed down my meal.

Once everyone returned from break it was time to go out on the floor to perform our hands-on skills. We were all to shower a resident. Luckily, we were able to complete the task in groups. Naturally, Harmony and I opted to work together. We were assigned to a soft-spoken peanut butter complexioned CNA named Treasure. She was a welcomed relief from Shaniece. Treasure gathered all of the supplies that we needed and brought in a wheelchair bound resident named Opal. Opal appeared confused, but pleasantly so.

We assisted Treasure with undressing Opal and transferring her to the shower chair. Fortunately, since this was our first shower experience, Treasure demonstrated and verbalized what we were to do. I honestly wasn't feeling being around Opal's old naked ass. Luckily since I worked the night shift, I was told I wouldn't have to do any showers. As Treasure went into detail about the importance of checking the water temperature, how many wash cloths were required and the order in which we were to wash different body surfaces, I started to smell something foul.

I scowled and pinched my nose as I watched a thirty inch soft served turd spiral from the bottom of the ass-less shower chair and plop onto the tile floor. I went into panic mode. While Harmony simply giggled, Treasure appeared completely unfazed. She didn't even acknowledge that anaconda! Once the shower lesson concluded, I couldn't ignore the elephant in the room any longer.

Clearing my throat, I asked, "Treasure, who is going to get the poop up off the floor."

She glanced at me with her poker face and replied, "You are. Grab some gloves and paper towels from over there." She pointed at the cabinet behind me.

I felt my heart racing and I felt faint. I had never picked up dog shit, let alone fresh human shit! I let out a long sigh and collected the gloves and paper towels as instructed. As I bent over, I gagged uncontrollably as the stench infiltrated my sensitive nares. This went on for a strong five minutes before Harmony gave me the evil eye and took over the task. The smell was so pungent that I had to leave that hot funky ass shower room and wait for the ladies in the hall.

As I stood there gasping for fresh air, our CNA Instructor, Jennifer approached me stating that it was my lucky day. She told me that postmortem care needed to be provided for a resident and to follow her. I didn't know what postmortem care meant, but surely it had to be better than the shit show I had just escaped. When we reached the outside of room 1313, I noticed that people appeared to be coming and going. Some looked as if they had been crying.

"Tonya, this is Junior. He is a NA (Nurse's Assistant) and he needs to be checked off on postmortem care. Can you walk him through the process please? He can assist you with transferring Mrs. Stewart from her recliner to her bed as well, before her family gets here." Jennifer rambled.

"Sure Jenn. I'll take care of him. Hi Junior. Are you ready?" She smiled at me brightly.

I said my hellos and told her that I was in fact ready.

Following behind Tonya, we walked over to a recliner on the far side of the room. There sat an elderly lady who looked…odd. Unnatural.

Being polite, I said hello to her. She didn't respond. Tonya gave me a look of puzzlement, but I chose to ignore her.

"Okay Junior, we are going to move Mrs. Stewart to her bed and get her cleaned up. Her family and hospice nurse are on their way up here." She informed.

"Okay." I replied.

"Usually we'd have to use a Hoyer lift, however, she is small so you can grab her upper body and I'll grab her legs. We can two man her into the bed that way. Hell, what can it hurt?" Tonya shrugged.

I thought it was strange that she spoke so candidly in front of the older woman, but who was I to question anything?

I stood at the top of the recliner and grabbed under the woman's arms. I looked on as Tonya grabbed her legs.

"Okay Junior, we are going to lift her on the count of three and move her over to her bed. Let's move quickly." Tonya commanded.

"Okay."

"One…Two…Three!" We counted in unison as we both lifted Mrs. Stewart with ease.

It was eerie because Mrs. Stewart's body remained motionless while her head turn at an odd angle and black shit spewed out of her mouth and onto the floor. Upon seeing this, I nearly dropped her ass because I didn't want that shit to get on me. It took everything in me to catch her upper half before she hit the floor head first.

"Junior, what the hell are you doing?! You almost dropped her body!" Tonya seethed.

Suddenly, it all dawned on me. Mrs. Stewart's ass was dead! This freaked me out so much that a flamboyantly guttural scream escaped my lips as I literally tossed the body onto the bed. I then ran out of the room and didn't stop until I found a bathroom. I leaned against the bathroom door and literally cried. Not an ordinary cry, but one of those ugly snot faced cries. What the hell had I gotten my stupid ass into?!

« Chapter 21 Sweet Cheeks »

AFTER THE POSTMORTEM incident, I was so embarrassed! Of course the news spread about how my ass freaked out being around that dead body. I had never experienced anything close to that before. I had never touched a corpse before in my life! For some reason, God spoke to me and told me to stick it out, so I did. The remainder of my orientation was fairly uneventful. I got along well with my nurses as well as the other CNAs. That is, except for Shaniece. That bitch didn't get along well with anyone. I just kept my distance.

Of course, I wasn't introduced to the beautiful world of Clostridium Difficile also known as C. Diff, until I was out of orientation and on my own. Nurse Vicky had given us report and she had alerted me to take special precautions when dealing with that particular resident, but I mentally was not prepared for the sight that awaited me. I knew there was some fuckery going on in room 1325 as soon as I walked in. The smell was unlike anything I had ever experienced.

I washed my hands, gowned and gloved prior to approaching the resident. I spoke to her and told her that I wanted to check her bed to see if she was dry. She was non-communicative, but I always talked to her anyway. Upon pulling back her covers, I nearly passed out!!! That woman was literally swimming in slimy, boogery shit! She had shit from her neck that puddled down at her feet! The shit was even on her hands. I pulled the covers back up and asked God for a sign. Surely, he didn't want me to continue working at that facility.

Receiving no signs, I poked my head out into the hallway and recruited assistance. It took us forever getting the poor woman cleaned up, but we did an excellent job. I battled the Diff all night long, but luckily none of her other explosions were as deadly as the very first. Throughout that night I contemplated different ways that I planned to kill Meelah the next time I saw her. Don't get me wrong, I appreciated the job, however, it was not at all what I expected.

My first paycheck warmed my soul! I had Harmony take me to a sleazy Buy Here, Pay Here car lot. I had to get my own ride. I had an extremely limited budget, so obviously my options were also limited as well. I found an old black 2007 Toyota Corolla for $250 down. Well actually, it was $500 down, but I flirted with the closeted car salesman and allowed him to brush up against my ass a few times. I test drove the car and it drove smooth like butter. I obtained insurance and happily waved Harmony off as I pulled away from the lot. I had my car!!!

I still hadn't heard from my dad or Jonah and wasn't really expecting to at this point. I had finally met my gorgeous niece and caught up on life with Aimee. She reported that my dad had developed a bit of a drinking problem and was openly running around with multiple women. He and Jonah were living as if our house was a bachelor's pad. Luckily in mama's will, she wanted her hidden savings to go towards paying off the remaining balance of the house, which was comprised mostly from the second mortgage.

This was a good thing because my dad wasn't able to keep steady employment due to his new bizarre behaviors. I suppose it was just his way of grieving. Aimee told me to contact mama's lawyer because she had divided her life insurance policy equally amongst us kids. Surprisingly, she left my father nothing except for the house. I had learned that her policy was for one-hundred thousand dollars which meant we each were to receive twenty-five thousand dollars! I know that math confused the hell out of you, but let me elaborate. Mama had even included Marlon in her revised will. He had actually replaced my pops.

Knowing this absolutely warmed my heart and spoke volumes as to what type of woman raised me. She was nothing short of incredible. After reaching out to the lawyer, he stated that mama had edited her will upon learning of my dad's affair and love child. She'd simply removed my father and added my brother in his place without a second thought. Unfortunately, there was a loophole that mama didn't foresee. With both Marlon and his mother being deceased, my dad was the next in line to receive the money on his behalf. He would receive the money anyway.

This irked my soul, yet according to the lawyer, it was not a battle worth fighting. He was certain that the ruling would be in my dad's favor. Aimee stated that she wanted to use her portion to move out and take care of Skyy. She'd told me that Nami had allowed Vasti's ugly behind to knock her stupid ass up. He'd apparently disappeared as fast as the second line appeared on her pregnancy test. I shook my head because another single mother was not what the universe needed.

She then told me that Corey had been by looking for me. Of course he had already received an earful from my dad about how my faggot ass wasn't welcome in his home. Deep down I missed him a lot, but he always dissed me to save face. Being his dirty little secret wasn't good enough now that we were adults. Hiding was no longer fun. Now that my family knew that I was gay, I didn't give a shit if the rest of the world knew about my sexuality. I didn't think that he was capable of being that free. He cared too much about appearances and insignificant people's opinion.

All I had were my memories of him and that big ass letter C to remind me of a love that I simply couldn't have. I brought Aimee up to speed on my new job and the crazy ass stories attached to it. I had her crying with laughter when I told her about the dead woman and the mega turd. She commended me and told me that she could never do that type of work.

I jokingly told her that she and I both knew that a person would do just about anything when their backs were against the wall.

Suddenly, she looked extremely sad and her eyes became watery.

I felt really shitty because I didn't take her feelings into consideration when I made that statement.

I guess it was too soon to joke about her druggie days. Those were the worse days my family had seen aside from mama and Marlon's deaths.

I embraced my big sister and apologized for hurting her feelings. Once she composed herself, she looked me in the eyes and told me never to apologize for speaking my mind. She then told me that she'd been through too much to experience hurt feelings. She said that she was simply reminded of how far she had come and how focused she had to remain to stay on track.

"Every time I look into Skyy's face, I know that I cannot afford to fail that child. I'm all she has." Aimee solemnly stated.

"Chick, you must be bugging! Never forget that she has me too. I'll give my life without hesitation for her."

"I know you would Junior. I don't have to ask you to take care of her if something happened to me, because I know that you would."

"Bitch, where are you going?! Are you trying to tell me something?" I asked becoming alarmed.

"No fool. I'm just saying. Mama's death really spooked me to the core. It brought my own mortality to the forefront of my mind. I think about when I was out there getting high and prostituting myself out all the time. I was engaging in some risky ass behaviors, yet God spared me and blessed me with a second chance named Skyy. I feel like mama and Marlon sacrificed themselves in order for me and Skyy to live. There were days when I begged God to take my life because I hated who I had become that much. I see now that my destiny was unfulfilled. He has bigger plans for me brother. For us!"

"Bitch, when did you become a motivational speaker?!" I joked trying to wipe away the stray tears that had escaped from my own eyes.

It was such a blessing having my sister back. The old Aimee before the drugs took over.

∞

"Heifer! Where is your upper body strength! I feel as though I am lifting this heavy ass mattress by my damn self. Lift!!!" I snapped at Meelah.

Today was moving day and the Texas heat was frying my black ass to a crisp. It should be illegal to be so damn hot! I was sweating from places I didn't even know I was capable of sweating from. Meelah, as strong as I knew she was, was lifting like an old lady today. Me, Meelah and Harmony had found a nice sized duplex that was renting out both units. I had Aimee check it out and she immediately fell in love with the place. I was going to love having her and my niecey pooh next door.

Her unit had two bedrooms and two bathrooms, while ours had three bedrooms and two and a half bathrooms. The front and backyard were a nice size. The first thing I did was ask the landlord if I could put a swing set in the backyard. I wanted Skyy to grow up with lots of good memories. It took me, Meelah and Harmony two days to put the swing set together. The look on Aimee's face when she saw what we had done was priceless.

Although she and Skyy had their own place, they spent the majority of the time over at our house. We loved every second of it. We were family and no one could break that bond. I was happier than

I had been since before mama's death. I had spent about five thousand dollars to get back on my feet. The rest of my money I planned to store away for a rainy day.

I needed a plan for my life. I still wandered if school was the right choice for me. I was not looking forward to the commitment attached to returning to school. My job was cool, however, I didn't see myself being there forever. I considered it a stepping stone much like IHOP. My love life was nonexistent. Both Harmony and Meelah were dating and while I was happy for them both, I couldn't help but to pity myself. I wondered if I'd ever find my soulmate.

Well, I believed that I had found him, but he kept slipping from my grasp. I'd often told Meelah that she was my female soulmate. If I ever settled down and was straight, I'd wife her up in a heartbeat. I was so thankful that our sexual rendezvous didn't affect our friendship. After we fooled around, we went back to business as usual. Neither of us ever brought it up and I would cherish our evening together forever.

After a lot of encouragement from my friends and sister, I decided to create a Plenty of Fish account. Yes…I was giving online dating one more chance. I'd definitely be much more cautious this time. I didn't have the confidence to meet and approach men in person, so I hoped meeting them online would come easier. I debated as to whether or not I wanted to post a face or a full body picture. I really didn't like the idea of me seeking out male companionship being broadcasted online. After much consideration, I decided to throw caution to the wind, and I posted a combination of face and body pictures.

My logic was, I never gave other profiles without pictures consideration, therefore I couldn't expect for others to seriously consider mine without them. Everyone who mattered already knew I was gay anyway, so I truly had nothing to hide at this point. I had used some of my savings and had hired a photographer to do a photo shoot to build up my portfolio. He had captured virtually every facial expression and pose that I was capable of doing. The pictures came out amazing. Of course, those were the photos that I opted to post to my profile.

I allowed my personality to shine through in the "about me" section. In no time, I had guys inboxing me. I was new to the world of online dating and it was exciting to be able to communicate with so many gorgeous men without any judgement. I got butterflies every time my POF app's notification feature alerted me of a new message. For approximately a week I would scour through dozens of messages, but not once did I respond. I was afraid to, primarily because of my last experience with Royce.

I knew my suitors would want to meet up and I didn't want to rush anything. At the conclusion of the first week, I deleted all of the guys that were not physically appealing or did not have a profile picture. Then I deleted those who lacked a mediocre vocabulary and simply messaged me "Sup". Next were those who requested "more pictures" or "dick pictures". Thirst always turned me off. My delete game was strong as hell. When it was all said and done, out of the dozens of guys who had reached out to me, only seven contestants remained standing.

After the highly anticipated wait, I decided to take the time to message each and every one of them back to see what they were about. When I attempted to contact two of the guys, I found that they'd deleted their account which was always a red flag. This left just five guys. I sent them all messages answering their questions and countering with my very own line of questioning.

Three of the guys appeared to currently be online, so I was hoping that their response time was better than mine. Two of the guys replied right away and we conversed for a while. The third guy had apparently read my message, but hadn't responded yet. I couldn't get mad because I had literally done the same thing. I had quickly learned that although the first guy to respond was sexy as hell, he was only looking for a quick nut. Everything out of his mouth was sexual and when we could "hook up". I blocked him and kept it moving.

The second guy who responded went by PopularLonerJay. My username was Sweet Cheeks. Gay as hell I know, but I literally couldn't think of anything else to express my sexuality. Plus, that's what my dad called gay men. I thought it was amusing. PopularLonerJay reminded me a little of myself in a sense that we were both young gay men struggling to find our places in the world. He was more or less looking for platonic friends to show him the ropes.

After conversing for a few hours, we finally felt comfortable enough to exchange our real first names. His name was Amir, but he insisted that I called him AJ. Checking out his profile pictures, he was light skin and had a muscular build. He had thick pink lips that were outlined by a neatly trimmed goatee. He claimed to be on the shy side and worked as a mechanic at a popular car repair chain. After getting to know AJ for a little while longer, it was time for me to get ready for work.

I promised him that I'd message him once I got settled in at work. I hopped in the shower and found my freshly ironed scrubs. Aimee always kept my clothes together for me just as mama did. I sprayed on my Paco Rabanne Invictus cologne and was all set for my night. My job preferred for us not to wear heavy scents, but I just didn't feel right without applying my "smell goods". All of the Edna's and Ollie's on my unit were just going to be choked up tonight! Hell, the nurses had medications to clear up any respiratory issues brought on by my fragrance tonight.

I grabbed my keys, wallet and gait belt and headed for the front door. Just as I opened it, there stood Corey looking like a snack.

I'm pretty sure I felt a small stream of drool run down my chin as I eye fucked him from head to toe. He was dressed casually in an oversized shirt and dark blue jeans, however, he instantly made my boy pussy jump. The fact that he smelled delicious wasn't helping either. Our sexual tension was so thick that it could be cut with a serrated knife.

I was so surprised by his presence that I didn't even notice that he had Shateara with him. She had gotten so big since I'd last seen her. Seeing her made my heart melt and just as quickly...I had fallen in love with him all over again. Seeing my baby girl took over my heart. I quickly took her from him and planted a kiss on her chubby cheek. I tossed her in the air a few times just the way she liked it and brought her tiny body in for the biggest hug. After showering my goddaughter with love, I finally directed my attention to her sexy ass daddy.

"Hey Junior, is Aimee over here? I knocked on the other door, but no one answered. She's watching Shateara for me tonight." He inquired in a sultry voice.

"Yeah, she's in the kitchen with Skyy. I didn't realize that the two of you were cool like that and that she baby sat for you."

"Yeah well I stopped by your dad's house a few times looking for you after you disappeared. Aimee was almost always the one to open the door when I stopped by. I didn't know where you'd run off to and I had to get your weekend with Shateara covered. I asked Aimee and she was happy to do it. She told me that she needed the practice anyway." He elaborated.

"Looking for me, hunh?" I asked raising an eyebrow.

"Not like that nigga." Corey chuckled prior to continuing.

"With everything that has happened within your family and the fucked up shit Jacoby did to you, I was worried when you went missing."

"You completely eliminated your contribution to my disappearance I see." I spewed with venom dripping from my words.

"What the fuck is your ass talking about man?"

"You know what? It doesn't even matter apparently. Like I said, Aimee is in the kitchen and I have to get to work." I replied feeling deflated.

Brushing past him, I looked towards where Shateara had been sitting so that I could tell her goodnight, but apparently, she had decided to explore our new house. As I was about to call out to her, Corey swooped in and tenderly pressed his lips against mine. I tried pushing him away because he'd just pissed me off, but he held me in place until I finally caved and melted in his arms. Being in his arms always felt so right organically. I'd never felt that way with Jean. I wished that I could remain in his embrace forever, but as usual, I knew that he'd have to return to his pseudo-heterosexual world. A world that excluded me.

I finally broke our kiss.

We stared at one another for what felt like forever before he said, "Look, I get it. I get it, okay? You are out and I think it's incredibly brave of you, but I just cannot give you what you want. At least not in the way you deserve it. I have a little girl that I have to think about. Plus, how would it look with me out here hustling in the streets to be fucking around with niggas out in the open. Come on Junior, that shit is bad for business."

"Are you freaking kidding me Corey?! After nineteen years of hiding this shameful secret, you want me to sneak around and go back into hiding like a little bitch? Hunh? A bitch…that's what you are

Corey. You and I both know that we are meant to be together, yet instead of acknowledging that truth, you want to keep living a lie. Who cares what those nosy pieces of shit think about you...me...about us?! They will gossip and talk shit no matter what happens between us." I spazzed.

"Junior, don't you ever call me a bitch!"

"Out of all the shit I just said, that's really the only thing that stood out?!" I said incredulously.

He walked over to me breathing heavily with a wild look in his eyes. He mean mugged me before saying, "Junior, count your lucky stars that I care about you. If I didn't, I would..."

"Corey, you'd do nothing to my little brother. You both need to cut it out. I have always known about you two. You both light up when you're in each other's presence. Corey, Junior is absolutely right and you know it. You are so worried about what all of these nonfactors out here will think that you are going to miss out on a good thing here. Life is too short to be out here bullshitting. Do what makes the both of you happy." Aimee preached compassionately.

"I...I...I'm sorry. I just can't. I won't." Corey said sadly.

"Well there we have it. It's nice to have it all out in the open so that I no longer have to wonder. I thank you for providing me with closure. From now on stop sending me mixed signals when you see me. As a matter of fact, stay the hell away from me! We are dead to each other. You got that?!" I growled poking him in his chest.

With that I stormed out of the house and furiously sped off towards my job.

« Chapter 22 Shitfaced »

LAYING IN A HOSPITAL bed this past week allowed me much time for self-reflection and discovery. Aimee's words about how short life is kept echoing throughout my mind and consuming my thoughts. While I personally felt that I was on the right track for someone my age, I realized that I could be doing so much better. It was time for me to step my game up and accomplish some of my goals.

While I was existing...I certainly wasn't living. I literally worked and went home every day. I was comfortable and content, yet not fully happy. Two days after my run in with Corey, I began to feel the classic symptoms of me going into sickle cell crisis. While I cannot solely blame him, I knew that he was a major contributing factor. I suppose I wasn't exactly taking proper care of myself either. The hospital had also diagnosed me with a urinary tract infection and severe dehydration.

I wasn't taking my maintenance medications as prescribed. My primary focus was working and keeping my head above water. I had woken up a week ago in excruciating pain. My back, hands and legs were killing me. My hands and feet were swollen up twice their normal size. The day prior, I had been a little fatigued and was running a low-grade fever, but I didn't think much of it. By the following day my temperature had skyrocketed to 102.8 and I hurt too badly to move.

Being the stubborn asshole that I was, it took my friends and Aimee the better part of the day to convince me to take my ass to the hospital. Of course I was familiar with lots of the staff there as they've treated me before in the past. They scolded me for not coming in sooner and also for not taking better care of myself. I was admitted immediately, and two liters of normal saline was bolused.

They put me on oxygen since I was sating lower than I

should've been, which I absolutely hated. You'd think I'd be used to it, but I hated having that tubing on my face. I was receiving Morphine via a PCA pump and I was squeezing that button every five seconds too. I was hurting so bad. I told Dr. Hampton that it felt like I was being stabbed from the inside in multiple areas. I wouldn't wish that type of pain on anyone. Well, maybe on Jacoby and Jean.

Speaking of Jacoby, apparently that asshole had shared our little video so much that it trended and went viral. I vowed to get revenge against that bastard if it was the last thing I did. After being in the hospital for a week, I was starting to come around. There was never a shortage of visitors. Aimee, Meelah and Harmony rotated shifts taking care of me and keeping my spirits up. Corey attempted to visit once and I promptly had his bitch ass escorted out of my room. I blamed him for this episode.

With me being out of commission, I spent the majority of my time conversing with AJ from the dating site. I ignored the other guys since I found AJ to be so interesting. Upon learning that I was in the hospital, he insisted on visiting me. I was hesitant at first for the obvious reasons. Then I realized that I was in the safest place to meet a virtual stranger. If anything went wrong, I'd swiftly press my emergency button. I hated that our first meeting would be with me being hospitalized, but his persistence eventually won me over.

I had Aimee bring me some clothes and I made myself as presentable as I could. Being out of that dreadful hospital gown instantly made me feel better. Having my own clothes elevated my mood and temporarily made me forget about being sick. I was still weak and had Aimee assist me into the chair next to my bed. I then kicked her out and told her to call me later for the *tea*.

No sooner than I did the breath test, there was a light knock on the door.

I let out a nervous, "Come in."

I held my breath as the door slowly crept open.

I bit my bottom lip as Garfield Bright's doppelganger came into focus. Damn! AJ was fine as fuck! Suddenly, I was feeling extremely self-conscious and was regretting our meeting. Surely he would glance at my sickly looking ass and high tail it out of here. Why would he bother taking on me and my baggage when he didn't have to. He could have his pick of men, why would he settle for my ass? Don't get me wrong, I was no slouch in the looks department, however, being hospitalized always brought out the worst in me.

"Junior? It is such a pleasure to finally meet you. Ummm ummm ummmph, you look even better than your photos." He stated sizing me up.

Although I knew he was full of shit, the attention made me blush anyway.

"Thanks AJ. It's nice to meet you too. Did you find the room okay?" I asked at a loss of what to say to him.

"It wasn't too difficult. Finding parking was the biggest challenge. Once I reached this floor, I just read the room numbers until I found you. I've been here before and this hospital is fairly easy to navigate through. Can I get you anything or do anything for you?" He asked handing me a get well bear that was holding three balloons.

"Awww that's awfully sweet of you. You didn't have to bring me anything." I gushed.

"I know, but I wanted to, handsome." He said smiling brightly.

He had the most perfectly spaced, white teeth I'd ever seen. Super white teeth on black men were the biggest turn on. AJ stayed for two hours before he headed out. He was so easy to talk to and down to Earth. Our chemistry flowed easily and you would have thought the two of us knew one another for years. I told him that I was hoping to be discharged within the next couple of days and then we could have an official date.

I was discharged three days later and it was so amazing being home. I had missed my own bed terribly. My job was extremely understanding about me having to miss out on work. I had enough PTO time banked to cover two of my days, but the rest, I was just shit out of luck. My check wasn't going to be shit, however, I still had plenty of money saved from my mom's insurance money, so I'd be fine.

I had missed my coworkers and my residents. I promised everyone that I'd be more conscientious about taking my medication and that I'd slow down working all of that overtime. I would work my forty hours a week and that was that. I would also take frequent water breaks throughout the day. I was getting stronger by the day. My first day back at work almost felt like a family reunion because everyone had showed me so much love.

I walked around hugging everyone and catching up on the latest tea circulating within the building. When I saw my absolute favorite resident Rosalind, my heart melted. She was sitting in her wheelchair dressed in the outfit I'd purchased for her a month prior. She came from a huge wealthy family who rarely visited her. Her clothes were all worn and too big, so I went out and purchased her three outfits with my money. I didn't mind and she looked beautiful. I guess her raggedy attire reminded me of someone...

When her eyes landed on me, somehow, she recognized me through her dementia and her face lit up. She couldn't really talk intelligibly, however, she did wave me over with her left hand. Her right hand was paralyzed from a previous stroke, so it lay contracted on her lap. It pissed me off because she did not have her brace on and her arm wasn't elevated as it normally would be. As I knelt down in front of her, she proceeded to playfully squeeze my cheek.

As soon as she finished, I smelt fresh shit and it was pungent. I immediately became enraged because I figured she'd been stewing in it for a while. I was going to have some choice words with her CNA. As I stood up, it was then that I realized that her left hand was covered in stool. I hyperventilated because I knew that it had to be on my face as well. I sprinted to the nearest bathroom to inspect the damage. My mouth dropped as I noted the fresh clay colored excrement on the left side of my face.

I gagged as the aroma infiltrated my nostrils. Rushing over to the sink, I proceeded to scrub the black off my face. My face stung from me crudely cleansing it with the facility's rough paper towels. When my skin had had enough, I knew then that I could no longer continue my career in healthcare. This incident made that abundantly clear. As much as I had grown to love it, this had crossed a line that I wouldn't soon get over. I was traumatized.

Walking out of the bathroom and down the hall was a blur. I felt sick for what I was about to do, but I could not get past having shit smeared over my face. I knew Rosalind meant no harm and was unaware of her actions, so I didn't have any ill feelings towards her. As if by fate, prior to me reaching the front exit, I noticed Imani pushing a resident in their wheelchair.

Reaching into my pocket, I grabbed ten twenty dollar bills. I had never talked to her much, however, on the rare occasions that we crossed paths, I always felt extreme guilt over stealing from her. As I neared her, she smiled at me. I smiled back. I reached for her hand and placed the money into it.

She looked puzzled, but I didn't care to elaborate.

I simply replied, "Thank you," as I continued on my journey out the front door.

« Chapter 23 Living My Best Life »

"JUNIOR!!! SOMEONE IS at the door for you!" Harmony yelled from downstairs.

I didn't have a clue as to who it could be as I didn't have many visitors. The only person whoever came by for me was AJ and he always called or texted beforehand. I lazily stretched and slowly made my way to see who was looking for me and most importantly, to see what the hell they wanted.

Opening the door, I noticed a well-dressed white woman smiling at me brightly. She had fiery red curly hair and kind hazel eyes. Trying to get back to binge watching American Horror Story, I didn't waste a moment with that heifer.

"Hi, I'm Junior and you are???" I inquired.

"Hello Junior, my name is Leigh-Ann Frasier and I am from L-A Modeling Agency. Is it possible to speak to you for a moment?" She introduced herself.

"Oh, my goodness! I know exactly who you are Ms. Leigh-Ann!!! Please come in!" I gushed like a groupie.

I led her into our family room and invited her to have a seat and she obliged.

"It's a pleasure meeting with you Junior and I'm sure you're wondering why I'm here. I received your portfolio and I must say that I found it very impressive. Very well put together. Well, as you may or may not know, we have merged with XXX Alphamales about a year ago. With that, we have successfully added some gorgeous male models to our team. Traditionally, we had only dabbled in the more conservative route, however, since joining forces with XXX Alphamales, we have expanded our already lucrative business into a goldmine.

I am seeking a different look. I'm so sick of seeing the same type of models over and over again. Now you, your face and your body are more aligned with what I am seeking. Your honey-colored eyes are strikingly beautiful. Your cheekbones and facial structure were made for the camera. You're small in stature, however, you are well toned and your washboard abs wouldn't require any airbrushing. Your chocolate skin tone will be unique as you will be our first African American model."

"Wow! Oh wow! I am so speechless. Why me? What does your offer entail?"

"You look exotic and I know that we'd be able to find you lots of work. Your earning potential for both the company and yourself is great. Now I must be honest, if it weren't for the popularity of your little video circulating out there, you probably would've been pushed to the side. My assistant, however, recognized you from the video and begged me to take a look at your portfolio. You would be expected to show some skin, and I do mean a lot of skin. Are you comfortable with that?" She stated.

"By skin, do you also mean…my meat?" I asked.

"Yes, if the other party requests it. Would that be an issue?" She challenged.

I thought about it for a few moments and replied, "No problem at all."

Leigh-Ann and I further discussed her offer which consisted of a ten thousand dollar advance plus two-hundred dollars an hour for photoshoots. I was elated. She left me a copy of the contract to read over and I promised to sign and return it within the next day or so. I couldn't believe that I was actually about to live out my dream of becoming a model. Even if I was an X-rated model. My salary was a hell of a lot better than it was working for the nursing home.

Life is funny sometimes. The same video that was created to destroy me, was the same video that was about to drastically change my life for the better. This was better than any revenge I could've concocted against Jacoby. I couldn't wait to share the news with everyone. I'd wait until everyone got home later to tell them the good news. I'd tell my boo in person after he got off work. Things were finally starting to look up for once in a long time. Me and AJ were growing closer by the day. He was so funny and considerate. He was always going out of his way to see that I was happy.

We'd been dating for a little over a month yet I'd felt as if I had known him so much longer. He typically came over and hung out with my friends and Aimee. He was really big into working out and maintaining his level of fitness which reminded me of Corey. Now that I'd be modeling, I was going to make more of an effort to start working out with him every day. I could stand to bulk up just a little. I didn't want to get too beefy.

I decided to go to the grocery store so that I could have dinner prepared for everyone once they got off. Since I was the only one not working and I loved to cook, I always made sure I fed my newly acquired family. Harmony was off today, but left out while I talked to Leigh-Ann to run some errands. We always ate dinner together and discussed our day. I decided on air fried pork chops, mashed potatoes, corn on the cob, green beans and homemade rolls. I also whipped together a strawberry cheesecake and grabbed a bottle of red wine.

Once dinner was complete, I hopped into the shower and dressed casually in my skinny jeans and an olive-green spaghetti strap shirt. Gucci sandals graced my freshly pedicured toes. Since moving in with my girls, they'd given me the confidence I needed to dress in what made me feel the most comfortable. I felt most comfortable wearing women's clothing, however, I never left home wearing them. I wasn't ready to make that move just yet. It was too dangerous for a person like me to prance around in women's clothing unprotected.

Slowly but surely everyone started trickling in from work. I knew they were suspicious of me because I simply couldn't stop smiling. I was on cloud nine and couldn't anybody take me down. At the dinner table Meelah opted to say grace. Afterwards we all began to eat and everyone graciously complimented the chef. I knew I had skills in the kitchen, but hearing them gush over my food was certainly an ego booster. Finally, I broadcasted that I had an important announcement.

"Okay ladies, the most wonderful thing has happened to me today! Leigh-Ann from L-A Modeling Agency stopped by and signed me to her agency!!! I am meeting with her at the agency tomorrow to sign and finalize my contract!!!" I squealed excitedly.

I had intentionally left off the fact that I'd be posing nude in the majority of my projects. It was neither here nor there. The details were insignificant.

"Seriously bro?" Aimee asked.

"Yes Aims! I finally made it!!!"

"Oh, my goodness! Congratulations boo!" Both Harmony and Meelah yelled while wrapping me up in a group hug.

"Thanks guys. I haven't told AJ yet, but I have a feeling that tonight might be the night that I bust it wide open for a real fella." I stated gyrating in my chair.

"Ewww bitch, you are so nasty!!! Harmony exclaimed rolling her eyes.

"Why you seem a little jealous over there Mony! You want some of daddy's dick before I go? That's a lot of ass that you're working with, but I'm up for the challenge heifer." I teased her.

I wasn't sure if it was the wine, but I could've sworn I saw Meelah roll her eyes. Since I wasn't completely sure, I decided to let it go.

∞

Later that evening, I was higher than a kite. I didn't smoke weed often so when I did, I felt that shit. I was in AJ's living room waiting for him to return from the kitchen with our munchies. I had him hooked on OITNB, so we were about to Netflix and chill this evening.

He returned with some cookies, popcorn, gushers and sprites. I was wrapped in a blanket waiting for him to join me so that we could snuggle. He climbed behind me on the couch and being in his arms felt like heaven. His fresh scent invaded my nose making my mouth water. I could never be in his presence without wanting to devour him. I told him about the modeling deal and he was ecstatic for me. I told him all the details and he was extremely supportive. He told me to pursue my dreams and to never live for anyone else.

He was absolutely correct. I had to do what made me happy. After a while I had completely tuned the show out as I felt his erection stabbing me in the back. I knew he wanted to remain the perfect gentleman and would never make the first move, so it was all up to me. Based on our previous conversations I knew that he was sexually fluid. He was open and versatile with his sexuality. He was open to being either top or bottom.

This was a new adventure for me because so far all the

guys I had encountered were toppers. I was finally about to poke something for a change outside of a runny pussy. Turning over to face AJ, I gently bit his bottom lip. This led to us passionately kissing. I absolutely melted under his touch. Breaking our kiss, I undressed AJ removing one article of clothing at a time. I smiled at his nakedness as I took in just how fine he truly was. I slowly snaked my tongue down his neck. He tasted so good.

I knew that he was enjoying himself by the low guttural growls that escaped from his throat. Moving down to his hardened nipples, I lightly pinched the right one as my tongue teased the left one. Finally wanting to enjoy his lollipop, I left a trail of kisses down his stomach and inner thighs. I took notice of how he had his dick and balls shaven. I could appreciate that. I don't think Jean ever owned a razor before. Maybe if he had shaved every once in a while, he wouldn't have had to force me to top him off.

AJ's meaty organ was standing at attention. He had a sexy veiny prick and the head mushroomed perfectly over the shaft. I spread his legs and elevated his ass on two of his couch pillows. Scooting down, I took his sack into my mouth. I lathered, hummed, licked and kissed his balls until he was throwing up gang signs with his toes. Grabbing his weighty dick, I flicked my tongue expertly along the underside of it. By this time, he was begging me to stop teasing him and to insert his erection into my mouth.

I was too happy to do it. In one swift motion, I swallowed all nine inches with lightning speed. Thankfully, I had no gag reflex because he was occupying my esophagus. I went slowly at first trying to become acclimated to his size. My saliva flowed effortlessly from my mouth and down onto his dick and balls. At some point, he grabbed the back of my head and began to rapidly thrust upwards into my waiting mouth. As he face fucked me, I inserted my index finger into his tight asshole and he instantly blew his load down my throat.

I had no choice but to swallow since his dick damn near reached my stomach directly. He may have been finished for now, however, I was far from done with his ass.

"Stand up." I commanded.

He did as he was told. I then bent him over his couch and used my spit to lube his winker. I instantly bricked up at the sight of his asshole winking at me. No man had ever offered up their lower orifice to me and for that, my feelings for AJ grew. I was as giddy as a kid in a candy store as I placed my tip at his opening. I felt his body tense a little, but relax as soon as I began to stroke his shaft. My eyes closed and my head fell back as I sank into the depths of pure bliss.

My dick had never been squeezed so snugly before. His tunnel was so warm and tight that I had to just remain stagnant for a few moments while I composed myself. When I regained control of my body, I began to wear his ass out. I power drilled into his body as he scratched at his couch. His moans were intoxicating. They let me know that I was hitting that shit right. Once he started throwing it back at me, I turned him over and threw his legs up on my shoulders and commenced to giving that ass the beating of a lifetime.

I popped a few of his toes into my mouth to stifle my moans. We were on the verge of waking up the entire neighborhood with our cries of passion. His sex faces were giving me life. I delivered AJ my best work and it showed. Both of our sweat covered bodies were glistening sexily in the darkness.

"Cum in me, Junior! Cum in this muthafuckin ass zaddy!" AJ bellowed.

That was it. I would've been powerless to hold back even if I tried with all of my might. I felt my nuts pulsate and I roared loudly as I released millions of my kids into his battered rectum. Feeling something warm on my abdomen, I glanced down and saw his volcano erupting for the second time that evening. Our eyes lustfully interlocked as I took my index and middle fingers and scooped up his seeds from my stomach. I then placed both fingers into my mouth moaning from his enchanting flavor.

I never wanted to leave his body, however, gravity defied me, and my limp member slipped out along with my sticky dew. He seductively used his rectal muscles to push my semen out of his ass. His hole was still gaping from the pounding it had just received. Seeing this, I felt my soldier stand at attention once more. It was then that I realized that we were in for a long night.

Laying on my back and stroking myself, I commanded, "Come and sit on it!"

I was definitely living my best life!

« Chapter 24 Elastic Heart »

"**JUNIOR PLEASE DON'T** be like that! I know things haven't been the greatest between you all, but they are still family. He is your brother and right now he needs all the love and support that he can get!" Aimee screamed with tears streaming down her face.

She continued, "Yes, I could put all the money up, but that wouldn't be fair to me now would it?"

"Aimee, your father and brother disowned me. Why in the hell should I go out of my way for either of them now? Where were they when I needed them? Hunh? I couldn't even go to my own mama's funeral Aimee! I had to watch the shit from a distance as if I were the paparazzi. It's fucked up that you'd even ask me to assist with anything concerning either of them!" I barked.

"Junior, you have the biggest heart out of everyone I've ever known aside from mama. I am asking you to help because I know deep down you still love them. You are bigger and better than our father and our brother. Everyone needs forgiveness sometimes. Look at me and what I've done to the family. I played a huge role in the way a lot of things have played out within our family. Where would me and Skyy be if you hadn't forgiven me?"

I thought about everything Aimee had said and as much as I hated to admit it, she was right. Apparently, my stupid ass little brother and a few of his friends were being accused of drugging and raping a cheerleader from their school at a house party thrown by none other than Jonah. As much as I wanted to distance myself from the entire situation, I knew Aimee and my mama in heaven would be so disappointed.

I guess my dad and Jonah had both blown through their life insurance money. Jonah was now eighteen and the accuser was a seventeen-year-old white girl, so the boys were facing some serious charges. His bail was set at one-hundred thousand dollars. He was also in need of a good attorney if he wanted a sliver of a chance of getting out of this mess.

Truthfully, my brother had always been a little asshole, however, he was certainly no Bill Cosby. I had been modeling for a little over five months and just as Leigh-Ann had predicted, I was an overnight success. I was raking in money hand over fist and now I was being asked to spend a huge chunk of it on someone who had counted me out. How ironic was that?

"Junior, do you hear me talking to you?" Aimee asked looking annoyed.

"How can I not hear you sis? You keep nagging me. Okay, I will meet with Jonah and if his story makes sense, I'll help him out. Don't think I'm showing up for his trial and shit because I'm not. I'll supply the funds only...fuck moral support. You can be that little spoiled bastard's cheerleader, no pun intended." I stated reluctantly.

I guess deep down, I didn't want my little brother becoming a statistic. I didn't want him to be another young black man occupying a jail cell. He was young and impressionable, therefore there was still room for him to grow.

"Ohhhhh thank you Junior!!! Thank you, thank you, thank you!!!" Aimee squealed.

I simply rolled my honey colored eyes and mumbled, "You're not welcome, heifer."

"I heard that Junior." My sister said as she playfully punched me in the arm.

∞

It was a Friday night and me, Meelah and Harmony had opted to step out and party at a new club called Tastys. Aimee wasn't much for the crowded scene and stayed home with my niece. I was wearing a black see-through shirt with some red leather pants. My eyebrows were arched to perfection and my nails were polished black. I had my mid-back length hair straightened with blonde highlights. My strawberry scented lip gloss finished my look.

Meelah was dressed in a burnt orange mummy style bandage dress with seven-inch nude stilettos. Her hair was styled in curly micro braids. Harmony's thick ass wore a purple backless shirt and the shortest pair of white shorts I'd ever seen. Her thick ass cheeks spilled out of the bottom leaving very little to the imagination. Her hair was cut into a short-spiked hairstyle that fit her face perfectly.

All three of us slayed and were ready to shake our asses on the dance floor. None of us were old enough to drink legally, so we were going to have to flirt and designate some sucker to get our drinks for us. Tastys wasn't a gay club, so I of course wasn't getting any play, so it was up to the girls to hydrate our livers. It didn't take long before a Sex on the Beach was placed in front of me. As I nursed my drink, I felt warmth on the back of my neck. Slowly twirling around on the bar stool, I saw a cute dark-skinned guy smiling at me. He was about five foot ten inches and was buff as hell.

His long dreads were in a neat bun on top of his head. He was cute and was dressed nicely, however, I had a man who was much much finer. I wasn't interested, but I suppose there was no harm in talking...right?

"Excuse me, Junior right?" He asked.

"Yep the one and only. How do you know my name?" I asked already feeling a buzz from the alcohol.

"Well, you are kind of a celebrity. I've seen some of your work and I think you're sexy as hell."

"And who might you be?"

"Oh, where are my manners? I'm Razz," He stated reaching to shake my hand.

"Nice to meet you Mr. Razz." I slurred being goofy.

He smiled brightly showcasing a very expensive grill. Normally I found them repulsive, but they suited him well. They made him sexier.

"Hey bartender, my friend's glass here is running on E." Razz stated ordering me another round.

Razz sat down next to me at the bar and we talked for a while about nothing in particular. I mostly watched the girls mingle and get their dance on. Razz told me that he was from New Orleans and was just in town for business. As he talked and told corny jokes, I noticed that he was becoming more and more handsy. I kept it cool and would politely remove his hand from my thigh or from my ass. I told him about AJ and he claimed to respect it, but his actions were saying otherwise.

After a few more rounds, I was over him showboating and

copping feels, so I thanked him for his hospitality and told him that I needed to relieve my bladder...which wasn't a lie. Trying to focus on his words over the loud music had given me a headache. I stumbled towards the restroom and was impressed by how clean it was.

"Hell, I'd take a raw shit in here. Straight cheek to seat." I mumbled to myself.

I pissed for what felt like an eternity. I finished by wiping off the tip of my penis and flushing the toilet. As I exited the stall, I saw Razz standing at the entrance looking at me seductively. I was no longer in the mood for his shit, so I rolled my eyes and headed over to the sink to wash my hands. I completely ignored his ass. As I worked up a good soapy lather, I felt myself being jerked away from the sink and slammed into a wall. I was roughly pinned face first into the wall.

I was beyond drunk and my strength was no match for Razz's buff bench-pressing ass. I had no fight in me, but I was able to plead for him to let me go. Either he didn't hear me, or he didn't give a fuck as he peeled off my leather pants. They were bunched up around my knees. I felt him rip my thong off and without any warning or lubrication, he roughly attempted to enter my anus.

I felt my asshole quiver as it rejected his invasion. I was screaming bloody murder and was praying that someone came to my rescue.

As if on cue, I vaguely heard someone yell, "Yo, what the fuck!", prior to me collapsing facedown onto the cold floor.

When I woke up, I was disoriented and felt like shit. My head was pounding, and I was relieved to be in my bedroom. Was it all a dream? It wasn't until I rolled over and saw a snoring Corey at the foot of my bed that I realized that last night was no dream. What the fuck was he doing here in my bed though?!

Being petty I started kicking him to get him to wake the hell up. I needed some questions answered and they couldn't wait for him to awake naturally.

"Yooooo, what the fuck nigga? Why the fuck are you kicking me and shit like you done lost your damn mind?!" He huffed.

"What the hell happened last night? Better yet, why are you in my room? I told you to stay away from me!" I snapped.

"Are you fucking serious? This is the thanks I get from saving your monkey ass from getting violated last night? A simple, thank you daddy would have sufficed."

"What happened last night? It's such a blur and my head is pounding."

"Where should I start? For starters, I am one of the owners of Tastys. I like to be behind the scenes, ya know. I was in my office watching the cameras, when I saw you and the girls walk in. I kept a close eye on the three of y'all throughout the night and zoomed in when I saw you entertaining that clown. I knew nothing good was going to come out of that situation. I kept my distance out of respect for your previous wishes. I didn't want to interfere with your life.

Instead, I watched your underage ass throwback glass after glass of alcohol. I knew that fool was up to some bullshit by the way he kept your glasses filled. You are an easy target and have to be more aware of your surroundings. After watching him cop some feels, I saw you stumble towards the direction of the bathroom. Not surprisingly, that clown soon followed. After about five minutes, curiosity got the best of me. I had a bad feeling in my gut.

I decided to investigate and came downstairs to see what was going on. When I came in the bathroom, he had you up against the wall with your pants down trying to shove his dick inside of you. I completely lost it when I saw what he was doing to you. I beat the brakes off that fool! Let's just say that my security made sure that he never does that shit to anyone else."

Tears were streaming down my face listening to Corey's account of last night's events. Why did I allow myself to get wasted enough for that to happen? I couldn't even remember what that asshole looked like. What exactly did Corey mean by his security ensuring that he never did that to anyone else? I wondered, but I would never ask. I was so grateful that he was there to save me once again.

"You were so drunk that I had to sling you over my shoulder and find the girls. Once I filled them in on what happened, they took off towards the bathroom and gave that muthafucka an even worse ass whooping before security could reach them. I drove you here, gave you a bath and put you to bed. You don't remember any of that?!"

I paused for a moment trying with all my might to remember his recounted story. Frustration took over my face when I came up with nothing.

Glancing at Corey, he could see my defeated expression. I suppose in an effort to make me feel better he took my left foot and started to caress it. Low moans involuntarily escaped from my swollen mouth. I guess I'd hit the ground pretty hard last night. I closed my eyes and drowned out the world as I felt my big toe being engulfed within Corey's moist warm mouth. I squirmed as his tongue snaked in between each of my toes, while he simultaneously hummed on them. I had never had a foot rub or had my toes sucked on before not even by AJ.

Oh shit! AJ! I had somehow managed to forget that he even existed. I was the world's worse boyfriend ever. Coming to my senses I remorsefully pulled my foot from his grasp and tucked it safely underneath my comforter. I was too ashamed to look him in the face, however, I could feel his eyes burning holes in the side of my face.

He then stood up and walked over to the side of the bed I was closest to. I don't know what it was about that man, but I somehow lost all control in his presence. I had made up my mind in that moment that if he tried to make a move on me, I wouldn't stop him. I had loved that man my entire life and even if I could never have him the way I wanted, I at least wanted to feel him just once.

His index finger caressed my chin prior to him lifting it, forcing me to peer into his beautiful chocolate eyes. In that moment, I could see all the love he had for me. I hated that he fought his feelings for me publicly. We were still teenagers, yet here he was part owner of a successful club and I was just starting what I hoped was a lucrative modeling career. Why couldn't he see that we'd be a power house together? Even Aimee could see it.

I shuddered when I felt his thick lips land on top of mine. I quickly recovered, ignoring the pain I felt from the pressure. Our tongues danced around one another. My breathing was haggard in anticipation of finally making love to Corey. Not breaking our kiss, I unfastened his expensive jeans and guided them off his body. I pulled his erection out through his boxers and my mouth instantly began to water.

I gently pushed him back so that I could look at what he was working with downtown. I was not disappointed. It was even more beautiful than I remembered. I completely sat up on the side of the bed with Corey standing between my legs. I leaned down and spit on his dick. Using both of my hands, I ensured that his tool was nice and slick before taking him into my mouth.

"Oh, my fucking…shit nigga!!!" Corey belted.

"Mmmhmmmmm." I moaned around his dick.

"Sssssssssss suck this dick Junior baby. Fuck! Suck this dick! You gonna let me fuck you, baby? I need to feel that shit today. I'm tired of the games. You gonna let me feel that joint, boo?"

I responded by sloppily slurping on his pipe. He tasted so good and I was in heaven as his ass muscles flexed. He was jackhammering into my face, yet I didn't mind one bit.

"Fuck Junior! Lay down now!"

I laid down. I was a bundle of nerves and I don't know why. Hell, I wasn't a virgin anymore. He climbed on top of me and lifted my legs in the air. I then felt his tongue dance around my asshole. I was lost in ecstasy and I didn't give a shit about who knew it. My trembling legs were suspended in the air as he made love to me with his mouth. I lost count of how many times I cried out his name.

When he finished, he came up and kissed me with so much passion that I couldn't catch my breath.

"Junior, a nigga has strong feelings for you. Fuck it, I love the fuck out of your ass. I may not be able to show you openly the way you would like, but there ain't shit I wouldn't do for you." He professed.

"You'd do everything, except be with me, right?" I challenged.

Sadness washed over his face, yet he said nothing.

He finally responded by placing his hardness at my entrance. My body instantly relaxed under his touch.

"Ummmm Corey. Fuck me right now! Fill this ass with that big juicy ass dick! I need to feel you baby." I cried out as he slowly inched his member inside of me making us one for the very first time.

Tears escaped my eyes and fell onto my pillow. I couldn't believe that this was finally happening between us. I'd wanted this very moment to transpire for the past few years and here it was.

I wrapped my legs around his waist and interlocked them at the ankles. I never wanted him to leave from my most treasured spot.

"Damn Junior...you feel so tight. Is this shit mine baby?" He asked stroking me in between each word.

"Yesssssssssss" I hissed.

"I can't hear you! Is this shit mine?!"

"YEEEESSSSSSSSSSSSS ZZZZAAAAAADDDDDDDYYYY!!!"

"Now that's better. Can I fuck you like this forever?"

"Ummmhmmmm...you can fuck me whenever you want."

"Ohhhhhh! You feel so good inside of me. I fucking love you Corey!" I cried out.

From the corner of my eye I was stunned when I saw an angry looking Meelah standing brazenly in my doorway. When she realized that I'd caught her spying, at first, she looked shocked. I guess when I didn't alert Corey to her presence, she became aroused. Her eyes became low as she lifted her nightgown up around her slim waist. The sight of her already bare pussy caused me to have a straight moment as I felt my dick somehow grow another inch.

Our eyes locked onto one another. She licked her fingers prior to placing them onto her swollen clit. Her nipples were hardened and visible under the thin material of her gown. As she quietly massaged her clit, Corey continued to bless my asshole stroke by stroke with his magic stick. After ten minutes, I felt his pace quicken, so I grabbed my pole so that I could release with him.

I soon heard him bellow, "Fuck baby, I'm cumming!!!"

"I'm cumming too zaddy!" I countered.

Prior to closing my eyes to brace for my release, I saw that Meelah too was shaking uncontrollably as a powerful orgasm tore through her chocolate body.

I experienced the most intense orgasm of my life in that moment. When I recovered, I noticed that Meelah was gone.

Had I imagined that too? Was I losing my mind? Two things were certain. First, I needed to stay away from Corey and secondly AJ could never find out about what had just happened.

« Chapter 25 Don't Mess With Texas »

DESPITE ALL THE MONEY and great lawyers that worked on my brother's case, he and the other boys were tried and convicted as adults. They were all handed two years sentences, which was a lot better than the thirty-year sentences that they were originally facing. Since none of the boys had prior offenses, they were let off somewhat easy. Apparently, the girl that they were alleged to have raped came from a very affluent family who had a higher reach than us. This was after all Texas, and not a lot had changed for people of color within the justice system.

The fact of the matter was, the girl was a hoe, and this wasn't her first rodeo with black cocks. The only difference this time was she actually liked my brother's black ass. She naively thought that if she threw her little pussy at him and his friends that my brother would want to go steady with her. Just as most boys his age would, he accepted the pussy and then treated her like the slut she portrayed herself to be afterwards. He wanted nothing to do with her.

Her ego and humiliation wouldn't let it go. Of course, the boys bragged to anyone who would listen. So instead of taking it as a hard lesson learned, she cried rape. There was no physical evidence since she didn't come forward until two weeks later. I still didn't associate much physically with my dad or my brother, but from what Aimee told me, our lawyers were brilliant in court.

The prosecuting team had nothing at all. Just the typical circumstantial evidence you see in the movies. The fact that the all-white jury found the group of black and Mexican teens guilty shouldn't have been too surprising, yet we were all genuinely floored by their ruling.

I would certainly be looking into an immediate appeal. It made me sad that justice was so poorly served in our case. Jonah along with the other boys would forever have to be reminded of that fateful night. They would have to register as sex offenders for life and live with the restrictions that came with the label. Throughout most of the trial I was traveling across the country working. Hell, I felt as if I were working for free since my brother's legal team always had their hands out.

Since I loved my brother and I believed in his innocence, I didn't mind covering his expenses. Money was money, I never developed an addiction to it like most people. It came and it went. I promised Aimee that as soon as I got in town, I'd visit Jonah. True to my word, I made arrangements to see my brother as soon as I touched Texas soil. Hopefully, we could repair our damaged relationship and become family again. Aimee and AJ had volunteered to make the three-hour drive with me to the prison. I was so nervous. I hadn't seen him in so long and I did miss him.

Arriving at the prison and looking at the old building was intimidating. I silently prayed that I never committed any crime serious enough to land myself inside of a place like that. The fences, barb wires and armed guards were everywhere. Here I was ready to run back to my car after just spending a few moments outside of the dreadful building. How was Jonah going to survive two years in this hell hole?!

"You do know that he is kept from the other inmates due to his crime, right? No one likes an alleged rapist, let alone a pedophile." Aimee spoke as if reading my mind.

"I don't think I can go in there Aimee. Look at this shit!!!" I exclaimed waving my arms around for emphasis.

AJ spoke up, "Baby, this isn't about you. Your little brother needs your support. I'm sure he is looking forward to all the love and support that he can get outside of this creepy place. The guards will keep us protected. No one can hurt you here Junior."

Oh, how wrong he was.

I skeptically glanced from Aimee and then to AJ before I mumbled, "Okay, let's do it. I'm ready."

"Yayyyy! Come on y'all." Aimee shouted excitedly.

Entering the prison was so invasive and demeaning. I felt so violated and couldn't imagine experiencing that process every day. The airport didn't have shit on that place. Luckily, I listened to Aimee and didn't wear anything too flashy or fancy. I didn't bring anything that would be considered contraband.

After being searched for what seemed like forever, we were led to a room where other families were waiting to visit their loved ones. The wait wasn't too bad. A huge smile spread across my face as I saw my little brother being escorted towards us by guards. My brother, however, wore a scowl on his freckled face. I didn't think much of it because he had never been a friendly looking person.

As he got closer, I heard him speak to Aimee...completely ignoring me.

"Yo Aimee, what the fuck did I tell you?! I told you not to bring these gay ass niggas up here!!! Your crackhead ass doesn't ever listen. I got enough problems and I don't want to be associated with these faggoty ass bitches!"

Aimee was crying like a baby at Jonah's hurtful words. I wasn't sad, however, I was homicidal.

"After all the money my faggot ass has spent to help you out, this is the fucking thanks I get you entitled little shit!!!" I seethed through clenched teeth.

"I didn't ask you to do shit for me. I don't want shit from you. You wasted your money anyway. I still got stuck in this hell hole, so don't stand there and act like your bitch ass has done me any favors Junior."

I was seeing red as images of me beating Jonah to death infiltrated my thoughts. I was tachypneic and my nares were flared larger than the R&B singer Mario's. Glancing down at my clenched fists, Jonah laughed.

"The fuck is your booty busting ass huffing and puffing at Sweet Cheeks? Nigga are you on your period or something?"

Seeing me ready to throw a punch, AJ grabbed me back.

"Let's just get out of here Junior. He isn't worth ending up in a place like this for. Fuck him...let him rot in this place." AJ said soothingly, while rubbing my back.

Something in his voice and the words that he spoke instantly calmed me down.

I smiled eerily at Jonah and deleted him from my brain and my heart. As far as I was concerned, both of my brothers were dead. Turning on my heels, I switched my pretty ass back towards the direction from which we came. I heard Jonah screaming for us not to come back along with other derogatory slurs. I was completely numb to his bullshit. Still, I didn't regret helping him as much as I had because I did it out of love.

His luck had unfortunately run out. I was officially done with him and not even Aimee or my mother's potential posthumous disappointment were enough to change my mind or my heart. He had just written a check that his ass couldn't cash.

"Don't drop the soap!" Were the last words I uttered to my brother before exiting the area.

Later that day Aimee had repeatedly apologized for Jonah's behavior. I told her that he was grown and responsible for his own actions. She needed to stop apologizing for him. She said that he always talked bad about me, but she thought he would've reacted differently seeing me in person. She was dead wrong. His ignorant ass had showed up and showed the fucked out.

I wasn't going to allow Jonah or anyone else to steal my joy. As much as I enjoy traveling the world and modeling for various big name companies, I always cherished my time with my family and friends. I always looked forward to being home. Harmony and her boyfriend Chaz had gotten a place of their own, so it felt a little weird being home without her. She was still working at the nursing home that I had met her at.

She was now in nursing school and I couldn't be prouder of her. Her thick ass was doing the damn thing. This just left me and Meelah in our unit. Aimee and my niece still lived next door. I did question Meelah about watching Corey and I and she simply shrugged. She really offered me no explanation other than sexing me every chance she could actually manage to keep my erection.

I was the worst boyfriend ever! First, I cheated on AJ with the true love of my life, now I was banging my best friend, whom I lived with every chance that I could. Her sexual appetite was insatiable and nothing was off bounds with her. She eventually professed her love for me. She didn't just love me, but she was *in* love with me.

After a while Meelah began to become petty and messy. She'd started making slick remarks in front of AJ. She'd always cop an attitude whenever he came over to spend time with me. I didn't know how to keep her happy while keeping our affair a secret. Aimee didn't even know that I was rearranging Meelah's reproductive organs.

Due to her erratic behaviors, I had begun to start spending more time over at AJ's place. This way I didn't have to worry about her throwing out her subtle hints. I can't say that I was in love with AJ, but he was my first real non-abusive gay relationship. He accepted me for me and he treated me like gold.

One evening before I was scheduled to be away on a three week assignment, I was lying in the prone position gasping for air. AJ had just creampied me and I was giving him a front row seat to my rectum regurgitating his cream filling. He loved watching it. As usual, we always fucked each other silly the night before my long stints away from home.

My body was sore and I was in dire need of some ibuprofen and a warm bubble bath. Once I caught my breath, I limped my ass into his bathroom and started the water for a long scorching bath. As I waited for the tub to fill, I walked over to his medicine cabinet to see what analgesics he had stored away.

Opening up his medicine cabinet, I noticed AJ had the usual items in there.

"Oh thank goodness." I said lowly when I spotted a bottle of Ibuprofen.

I rolled my eyes when I noticed that they'd expired four months prior.

"What the hell can it hurt?" I shrugged swallowing four of them without water.

As I went to replace the medicine bottle, curiosity got the best of me as I noticed two prescription bottles with AJ's government name printed on them. They stood out because the rest of the bottles were in over the counter bottles and easily identifiable as vitamins.

Retrieving the two bottles, I proceeded to read the printed words on the bottles. The first one read Levothyroxine. That didn't ring a bell at all. With my mom being a nurse, I would sometimes read her medication books when I was bored. I made a mental note to google the drug after my bath.

I replaced the pill bottle in its original spot in the medicine cabinet. I then grabbed the second bottle. Its label read Truvada. Now that drug name looked familiar...but why? I stood there trying to remember where I'd heard of the drug before, when I suddenly felt as if I couldn't breathe. The reality of that drug's most common use had me feeling faint.

Every commercial I'd heard advertising Truvada came flooding through my ears.

"Oh my God! He has HIV!" I screamed at the top of my lungs.

Collapsing to the floor, I ignored the banging on the other side of the locked bathroom door. We never wore condoms...did I have it too? Did I give it to Meelah? To Corey???

« Chapter 26 To Prep Or Not To Prep »

"WHAT THE FUCK JUNIOR! Chill the fuck out, baby. What is up?!" He yelled.

"Get your muthafucking hands off me you dirty dick having muthafucka!!!" I spazzed.

"What the hell are you talking about a dirty dick for?"

"You have a dirty dick bitch! You have AIDS! I saw your medication in the bathroom!!!"

"No, you got it all wrong, boo! I do not have HIV...nor do I have AIDS! I have Truvada for PrEP prophylactically. I swear to you. I do not have HIV or anything else for that matter. I would never do that to you baby. I'm just protecting myself, since it's been proven to be so effective."

"Fuck you! I don't believe shit that you say. You'd say anything. It's over and if you gave me anything, I will be pressing charges!!! Now move, I'm leaving!"

"Baby please don't do this. You are wrong. I'm telling you the truth. I get tested every six months. I was tested two months ago. Would you like to see my test results?" He inquired.

I had managed to calm down a little bit. At least long enough to finally comprehend his words. My silence prompted him to walk off in the direction of his office. I took that moment to get dressed. I needed air and space. As I slid on my shoes, AJ returned holding a piece of paper.

He looked disappointed and defeated. He walked over to

me and handed me the paperwork. Everything was as he said it would be, down to the date. Despite reading that he was HIV negative, I still felt uneasy and confused. I didn't know what to believe. Pushing the document back at him, I stormed off in the direction of his front door.

Thankfully, he didn't try to stop me. I was able to exit without any more drama. I needed to get to the closest Walgreens. I wanted to pick up one of those rapid HIV kits called OraQuick. With me going out of town in the morning, it would have to suffice for now.

Although I was bringing home a nice salary, I continued to live within my means. I loved all of the fancy clothing that I modeled in, however, unless it was gifted to me, I personally didn't buy any of that high-end stuff. With that being said, OraQuick kits were expensive!!!

While Walgreens sold the kits individually, I opted for the one with 3 testers. I had to be sure. My drive home was the longest one ever. It was a miracle that my ass wasn't pulled over. Barely turning my ignition off, I leaped from my car and darted up the front steps leading to my house.

Unlocking the door, I could smell some good food being cooked. Normally I'd investigate, but right now I was on a mission. I was possibly dying, so my stomach could wait. I was shaking with each stair that creaked under my weight. Making it to the landing, I opened my bedroom door.

I rolled my eyes when I noticed Meelah sprawled out in a sexy pose on my bed.

"Meelah, what the hell are you doing in my damn room? What if I had AJ with me?! I don't know what has gotten into you, but this thing between me and you is over. I want that old thing back. I want my friend back." I stated urgently, yet compassionately.

A deranged wild look took over her face before she threw her head back in laughter. She almost looked and sounded possessed. All I could think of was getting her goofy ass out of my room so that I could tend to my business.

'You are what has gotten into me Junior! I love you. I've always loved you even with you constantly friend zoning me. I've always had your back...more than even your family has. I've fought bitches for you. I've been arrested for you. I've held you down when you were broke and homeless. I've hooked you up with a job."

"Name one muthafucka in this world who has held you down more, aside from your late mama. I'll wait nigga..."

After her petty ass waited for what I guess was a full minute she continued, "That's exactly what I thought. I've full heartedly accepted you for being you. I know that you're into guys, but I've also proven that you can be attracted to and turned on by women too. Your body responds to me unlike when you were with Nami."

I looked at her as if she had lost her mind, although everything she had just mentioned was true. I couldn't argue with any of her points.

"So, what are you saying Meelah?"

"I'm saying that I want you to leave AJ and give us a fair shot. I love you."

"Wow, why are you just telling me all this now?"

"I never wanted to fall for you. I wanted you to be happy and I never wanted to interfere with that. As I fell in love with you it became more and more difficult. After we made love, although, it was brief...it became impossible for me to be happy for you loving someone else." She confessed.

"You don't need to give me an answer now. Just think about it Junior."

I threw her a genuine smile and replied, "That's fair enough Lah Lah."

"Excuse me, I need to use the bathroom." I told her.

I heard everything that she'd said loud and clear. As far as I was concerned, me and AJ were over. There was no repairing that relationship. But did I want to get caught up in yet another heterosexual relationship that I didn't want to be in? Meelah and I had a much deeper connection than what I had with Nami, so maybe this time around it would be different.

Meelah waved me off excusing me. I headed towards the bathroom. My old anxiety began to resurface as I remembered what I needed to do and also what was at stake. My future...my fate was in the bottom of the flimsy Walgreens bag that I carried.

Was this really my ending? Was an AIDS-related illness going to be typed on my death certificate? I couldn't help but to be embarrassed as I envisioned the medical examiner standing over my corpse in silent disgust. All healthcare professionals had their stigmas and the majority hated dealing with HIV/AIDS patients, but most would be reluctant to verbally admit it.

Entering my bathroom, I quickly shut and locked the door behind me. I walked over to the sink and was baffled by the clutter. I hadn't left my bathroom that way. Why had Meelah been in there when she had her own bathroom?! As I went to remove the bullshit that she had sprawled out all over my sink, something caught my attention.

As I visually focused on the items in front of me, my mouth dropped. This shit seriously couldn't be happening tonight. Tonight of all nights!!!

Tears fell down my face as I processed what Meelah was telling me. There were exactly twelve positive pregnancy tests before me. They varied in brands and delivery. Some simply had two lines, some had plus signs, a couple broadcasted smiling faces while the rest boldly read PREGNANT.

I was going to be a father. I placed my bag underneath the sink in my bathroom and emotionally walked back out and reentered my bedroom. Meelah wore a nervous expression on her angelic face. I looked intensely into her dark brown chinky eyes for a few moments. With my eyes, I beckoned for her to confirm what I already knew to be true.

Slowly nodding her head, a huge smile spread across my face. Seeing this, relief instantly washed over her face. I speed walked over to her. Kneeling in front of her, I wildly kissed her all over her face.

The room quickly filled with her laughter. Her laugh always brought me joy. I missed that laugh. Her smile lit up any room. Being gay, I never thought that I would ever experience parenthood. Now was not ideally the best time to be bringing a baby into the world, but I had no regrets. I was having a child with my best friend.

Laying her back onto my bed, I placed each of her thick legs onto my shoulders. I then slid her pink panties to the side and dove head first into her ocean. I had pushed the OraQuick test to the rear of my mind. My priority in that moment was to orally please my soon to be child's mother. Tomorrow was another day. If I was dying, finding out a day later wouldn't make that much of a difference.

« Chapter 27 Branded »

AFTER BLESSING MEELAH'S pearl and walls for hours until she fell asleep, I decided to follow her lead and laid down beside her. There was so much on my mind, however, exhaustion won over and I too was snoring. I had an early flight to catch the next morning and I didn't want to show up to my next shoot with bags under my eyes.

I woke up a few short hours later with a heavy heart. I truly wanted to do what was best for me, my unborn seed and also for Meelah. As soon as I stood to my feet, her eyes snapped open. I threw her a smile. I told her that I needed to shower if I wanted to catch my flight on time.

Before entering the bathroom, I looked over my shoulder and asked her why she'd taken so many tests.

"I bought twelve because that's the number of times we've made love, Junior. That's twelve possible times we've had to conceive our baby."

I nodded and proceeded to the bathroom.

As the hot water beat down on my body, it was then that I made a decision. I was going to try with every fiber in my body to put my love for men behind me. Even if I lusted after men, I didn't have to act on the shit. I was strong-willed and capable of anything.

I wanted to do right by Meelah, because she deserved it. I still had so much love in my heart for Corey, but I knew he could never give me what it was I deserved. After he saved my ass that night and we had sex for the first time, he all but disappeared. I was so over his scary ass. Why hide in shame when I could be so open and free with my best friend?

After my shower, I got dressed, kissed Meelah and her flat belly. I then took off for the door with my suitcases in tow. My flight was smooth as butter. I arrived in Atlanta just hours later. It would be my home for the next couple of weeks. My agency had gotten me a room at the Ritz and I was in awe.

Lounging around in my robe, I remembered my OraQuick kits. I walked over to my suitcase and retrieved the box. I read the instructions on the back of the box and set up the first test. It was easy to follow. I took the test stick and swiped it against my upper and lower gums once. I then stuck my test stick into the solution.

It was then that I set my alarm clock for twenty minutes. I held my breath the entire time...at least it felt that way. My palms were sweaty. My chest was tight and my heart was palpitating. When the alarm sounded off signaling my wait was over, I suddenly developed the bubble guts.

Ignoring my gurgling intestines, I sat up and peeked at my results. I released a long sigh of relief as I noticed only one pink control line. There was not a second line next to the test area. This meant that I was HIV negative! I let out a bizarre mixture of a laugh and cry. I was going to live to raise my baby after all!

Now I'm not ignorant. I know there are many people who live long productive lives with the advances in the HIV medication. However, there was still a large population of people who were resistant to those drugs and their HIV quickly advanced to full-blown AIDS. I supposed I owed AJ an apology for my behavior and for not hearing him out.

Picking up my phone, I called him. He picked up on the first ring.

"Hello, Junior. Baby, are you there?"

My voice cracked before whispering, "Yes I'm here."

"I've been so worried about you. Where are you?"

"I'm in Georgia."

"I'm so sorry that I didn't tell you that I was on The PrEP. I guess it was a conversation that should've been had."

"Yes, I agree. I called to tell you that I'm sorry for reacting the way that I did. I'm also sorry for not hearing you out. I saw that medication and my life flashed before my eyes."

"Apology accepted. None of that matters. When are you coming back home?"

"I'll be home in two weeks."

"When you get back can we talk?"

"Sure, but I gotta get ready to go now. I'll talk to you soon."

"I love you Junior."

My eyes watered as I tearfully hung up.

I wanted to tell him about Meelah and our baby, but I'd give him enough respect to have that conversation man to man.

∞

During my stay in Atlanta, I had taken the remaining OraQuick tests just to air on the side of caution. They too were negative. God was good. I was able to finally relax and enjoy some of the city's, festivities. The night life in Georgia was unlike anything I'd ever experienced. On my fourth day in Atlanta, I was dressed up as a Trans for the shoot.

While I have previously dressed up in mama's clothes growing up, I had never had professional makeup done. With my soft feminine features, no one could tell that I wasn't born with a pussy between my sweet thighs. I was so gorgeous. I was never a hairy man to begin with. I never grew much facial hair and my chest and back was hairless.

My jaw line was soft and rounded like a woman. My naturally arched eyebrows would make Queen Bey herself proud. My smooth dark skin and honey colored eyes were striking in itself. I had a nice size ass for a guy my size.

One of the other models that were in my shoot had asked me to hang out with her after we concluded our session. I was hesitant at first as I didn't really know her or the city well. I typically liked to be strictly business during my work trips. Isabella was extremely persistent and I finally agreed to accompany her to a popular night club.

I was going to behave myself and I had no intentions on drinking at all. It was warm, so I had a short white form fitting dress on with a pair of red bottom shoes that was gifted by one of my admirers. One of the many perks of being a model was the endless gifts. My makeup was still intact from my shoot earlier and my wet and wavy lace front wig had me out here looking like Chilli from the group TLC.

Isabella was transitioning into a woman and had gone as far as to have breasts implants, lip augmentations, a Brazilian butt lift, cheek implants and was on hormones. Sadly, even with the small fortune she'd shelled out, she still wasn't convincing. She was six foot four and her body was a little too buff. She also wore just a tad bit too much makeup. She looked unnatural. She appeared to try too hard to be a woman.

She was cool nonetheless. She was flamboyantly fabulous. She enjoyed being the center of attention. I just wanted to be low-key. The club Isabella drove us to had all walks of life there. The music was upbeat and the smell of marijuana and must permeated the stuffy air. It really wasn't my crowd, but I decided to seize the moment.

I danced with a few thirsty dudes, however, I couldn't be sure if they were aware that I was biologically a man, so I didn't get too carried away with any of them. A lot of people in the LGBTQIA community had lost their lives over tricking others'. This was my first time coming out of the house dressed as a woman and I was extremely nervous. I knew I was playing a dangerous game, yet I'd never felt more myself.

After a while, I started getting an eerie feeling. A feeling as if I were being watched. I scanned the club, but saw no one paying me any mind. I brushed the feeling aside. I ordered some hot wings and fries with a glass of water. I figured it was as safe as safe could get. I knew better than to turn away from my drink even for a moment.

My hot wings came and my mouth watered. I always ate very little close to and during my photo shoots. I would just have to pick up a bottle of magnesium citrate when I got out of there. I wasted no time digging in. I greedily smacked on my food, leaving not even a sliver of meat on the bones. I then scarfed down my fries in an attempt to cool down my scorching mouth.

Satiated, I sucked on my fingers one by one savoring the spicy flavor that clung to them. Squeezing my lemon over my chilled water, I swallowed its contents in one huge gulp. I was full and now that itis was settling in.

"Oh shit! I hope that I didn't fuck up my lipstick!" I spazzed to myself.

Removing my compact from my clutch, I inspected my face, particularly my lips for smudging. I was impressed when I noted that my lips were still the same shade of red as they were earlier in the day.

"What type of lipstick is this?" I wondered out loud.

As I went to close my compact, the image behind me stopped me in my tracks.

Standing behind me was none other than Corey with Isabella.

Slowly turning around, I could tell that Isabella was hammered.

"Here's the friend I was telling you about! Isn't she absolutely gorgeous?!" Isabella slurred.

I watched Corey's eyes to see if they held a flicker of recognition or surprise, yet I saw neither.

"Damn, you were right." Corey stated licking his sexy lips.

I couldn't help, but to blush.

"I'm Corey." He announced with his hand extended for a handshake.

"They call me Merlana." I said in the most feminine voice I could conjure up.

"Nice to meet you sexy Merlana."

"The pleasure is all mine." I flirted.

"I guess I'll leave the two of you alone now." Isabella interjected.

The club was pretty dark, so I used that to my advantage. I tried to avoid eye contact and kept my head turned at an angle to avoid detection. What were the odds of me running into this fool in the ATL of all places? This shit was getting spooky. After this, no more clubs for me!

I couldn't believe that he didn't know who I was. Makeup or not...I felt that he should've recognized me. Felt my presence or something.

We conversed for a few minutes over the loud music. He then invited me upstairs to the VIP area. It was so nice up there. Then again, the entire establishment was pleasing to the eye.

"Follow me, Merlana."

I trailed behind him taking in the scene. People were getting frisky up there. The smell of expensive liquor and sex intruded my sensitive nose. What type of shit was Corey into here?

We ended up on the outside of a large steel door. He swiped his hand across the sensor and the heavy door slid to the side, granting us access. My mouth dropped as soon as we entered his large office. Corey had certainly come a long way. I bet none of the people around him now would believe his humble beginnings story. I was so proud of him.

"Would you like a drink beautiful?"

"Naw, I don't drink." I refused.

"Aight. Want to listen to some music?" He asked grabbing the remote to his stereo system.

"Sure, can we listen to Sade or Floetry?"

"Hell yeah, I got you boo."

I just flashed him a shy smile.

He sat on a long leather crème colored couch, while I sat in the matching loveseat. He stared at me for a few moments before sparking up a fat blunt. He took a few pulls as he concentrated on me. I was feeling self-conscious by the way his eyes tore threw me. His eyes were sexily dropping lower and lower to the point that I wondered if he could still see me.

"Why are you all the way over there, ma? Come sit next to me."

I hesitated for a minute, but then slowly got up and walked seductively over towards him. As I went to sit down, he palmed a handful of my ass, causing me to slap his hand away.

"My bad ma, that shit was looking too juicy for me to resist. Don't be scared, I'll behave."

I cautiously sat down beside him.

"Do you want to hit this shit?"

Ordinarily I would say no, but since it was Corey, I could trust him to make sure no harm came my way.

"I'd love to." I said in my Texas drawl.

He held the blunt up to my lips and I pulled on it, instantly feeling its effects.

"You look so familiar Merlana, but I don't know why. Are you from the ATL?"

"No, I'm from all over daddy."

He smirked and said, "I love a mysterious woman."

My heart sank a little bit because I knew that I was not at all what he thought I was. He was looking forward to some pussy, but all I had to offer was some *boy* pussy. I knew it was time for me to go before he realized that I was in fact a he and not a she.

"Thank you for the hospitality, but it's time I got going. I have to work early tomorrow." I replied standing up.

"No, stay." He commanded reaching for me and sitting me on his lap.

I tried to hop up before his hands could roam over my body revealing my secrets. It was unfortunately too late. His hands were already sliding up my dress and groping at my bulge. I froze waiting for his reaction. I closed my eyes anticipating fists to fly, however, I was gently being laid down on the couch. My skimpy dress was being pulled up to my silicone filled bra. I then felt a finger tracing my lower abdomen.

"I knew it was you, Junior. Your presence, your scent, your voice...literally everything about you. Plus, I'd recognize that tattoo anywhere." He seductively growled pulling my thong off.

« Chapter 28 Second Chances »

"JUNIOR! STOP BEING SUCH an asshole! Please drive me to the hospital! I am shaking too bad to drive myself!" Aimee screamed at the top of her lungs.

I was minding my own business spooning with my soon to be baby mama and she was interrupting my beauty sleep.

"Leave me alone, Aimee. Order you an Uber if you can't drive! Fuck that bastard! He is already dead to me!" I snapped.

I instantly felt like shit as I felt Aimee's small body drop onto the bed beside me and violently shake as she sobbed. I finally turned over to look at my sister and she was seriously distraught over our bitch ass father. Apparently, he had developed diabetes and was in a diabetic coma. He came in to the ER with a blood glucose of 806. One of the many women that he had shacking up in my mama's house had called for an ambulance after finding him cold, clammy and unresponsive.

While that was pretty noble of her and shit, the bitch failed to stick around. The raggedy bitch booked it prior to the ambulance arriving. My dad didn't have a lock on his phone, so the hospital was able to track Aimee down by his contacts. I highly doubted that I was still saved in his phone. Truth be told, I couldn't care less. The hospital apparently called her and got her all upset.

Now she wanted me to get up out of my comfortable bed to see about his monkey ass. I didn't care if he lived or died. Neither his life nor death would impact my life one way or the other. But damn, Aimee and my niece were my weaknesses. As she cried over that foul sorry excuse for a father, I knew I'd be getting up soon to take her to the hospital. It was going to be a long ass day!

After throwing on some clothes, I kissed Meelah and Skyy on their foreheads and took my sister to check on Merlon Sr. On the ride there, she squeezed my right hand so tightly as she continued to weep. I dropped her off in front of the hospital and promised that I would join her shortly. I found a spot inside of the parking garage and prayed for the strength to make it through the day.

I exhaled as I exited my vehicle. I took the elevator up to the second floor. I asked the ICU nurse where I could find my dad and sister. She gave me the room number and I slowly headed in that direction. Once outside of his room, I braced myself for the chaos I assumed was beyond the sliding glass door. I slid the door open and could hear my sister crying beyond the curtain.

I know it was ignorant of me, however, hearing my sister so upset made me more pissed off at my dad. I hated to hear her cry. I spotted her sitting in a chair next to his bed holding his hand. He was hooked up to all kinds of IV bags. He had on a nasal cannula. He looked so thin and frail. His light skin was ghostly pale. A Foley catheter bag was filled with amber colored urine and a flexi seal bag contained my father's stool.

Between the visual and the constant beeping and whooshing of machines and monitors, I too became a little choked up. I hated myself for even caring about him. My heart was bigger than even I wanted it to be. I was frozen in place and unable to move any closer. Aimee prayed over our father and begged for him to be strong. She willed him not to die and told God to hold off on taking him home.

"I know you're not perfect, but you are the only parent we have left. We cannot lose you, too. Be strong for us daddy!" She cried.

Tears involuntarily graced my cheeks. I wanted to run from the room. This was just entirely too much. The nurse and doctor came in and explained everything that was going on with him. He was in critical condition at that time. He was slowly receiving IV insulin to help reduce his glucose levels and thankfully it was coming down. Normal brain activity was detected, so it was up to our father as to whether or not he was to pull through.

That wasn't even half of it. He was also septic from a necrotic left foot wound and running elevated temperatures. He was receiving several intravenous antibiotics to combat his raging infection. The ABI test to his left leg showed that there was virtually no blood flowing to it. It had to be amputated. The doctors didn't want to wait and put the ball in our court. It was up to Aimee and me to decide whether my father was to lose a leg or lose his life.

Times like this made me miss my mama even more. I wished that we could delegate that decision to her. After much thought and consideration, we sided with life over limb in the end. The surgeon stated that if my father broke his fever and was still alive by the next morning then she would operate on him. Aimee and I held vigil at his bedside throughout the day and night.

AJ came and paid his respects as well. He and I had agreed to be friends after the little Truvada mishap. I also found out that the other drug, Levothyroxine was for his thyroid. I confessed about cheating on him and having a baby on the way with Meelah. He told me that he couldn't get past me having a baby on him and also for putting *him* at risk. I completely understood where he was coming from and we both moved on.

My dad's temperature was monitored through the night and miraculously each time it was checked, it had decreased. By the time the morning rolled around, his temp was sitting at a perfect 98.6 F. True to her word, the surgeon approved my dad for his surgery. For two hours I watched as Aimee paced back and forth. After a while, the surgeon emerged with a poker face. We weren't sure if he had survived the surgery or not. Dr. Spencer told us that it could go either way.

"Hey, you two. I am happy to report that your father faired just fine. He is still out of it, but hopefully having that toxic foot removed will help his body recover that much faster. Give us about thirty minutes or so to get him into the recovery room and then you can go and see him. From the look of his foot, he's had diabetes for an extremely long time. I'm shocked the military didn't catch it. Take care of him. Oh and don't forget to take care of yourselves." Dr. Spencer said and then retreated back behind the double doors.

∞

My dad's surgery was six weeks ago and he was progressing beautifully. He went to a skilled nursing facility for a while as they helped him recover. His stomp was still too fresh for a prosthetic leg to be fitted and worn. He was really looking forward to getting up and walking again. He was in a wheelchair for now. I honestly thought that he would hate Aimee and I for deciding to have his leg amputated.

He reported speaking to mama and God when he was on the brink of dying and he didn't like what he had become. He said mama was so disappointed in him for how he turned his back on me that he could barely stand to look at himself. He knew it would take a lifetime to make it up to me. He begged to be given a second chance to right all of his wrongs and it looked as if he had been granted that opportunity.

He stated that his first mission was to get all of his kids back on good terms. He knew that he heavily influenced a lot of Jonah's homophobic thinking, so he was certain that he could persuade him back in the other direction. He made us all return to the prison and hash out our problems. Sadly, my little brother arrived to the meeting with his now long reddish hair in a ponytail and his face was painted in prison made makeup.

He looked so sad and I was sad for him. Me and Aimee burst into tears at the sight of him. Despite all the hurtful things I had said to him, I'd never want anyone to be raped and turned into someone's bitch. We immediately reported what was happening to the warden and my brother was placed into protective custody pending a transfer a little closer to home. Seeing his sad demeanor also prompted me to begin financially helping him again. I had filed for an appeal on his part. I wouldn't quit until he was freed.

Luckily, his sentence wasn't lengthy to begin with, however, even if he was released just a day early, it would be worth it. It was nice to be rebuilding a relationship with my family again. Meelah's baby bump was growing by the day and I couldn't wait to meet our daughter. We had decided to name her after my mama and Meelah's grandmother, who helped raised her while her mom was out drugging. Melanie Rose Hilton was our daughter.

∞

I was blowing up in the modeling industry. I was no longer limited to just smut. My face graced the cover of many of the major magazines. I even received small supporting roles alongside some major hitters in the acting scenes. I was the face of the LGBTQIA community. We were far from rich, however, we were not wondering where our next meal was coming from. I was still not a frivolous spender. I penny pinched and bargain hunted when able.

The one exception was when it came to shopping for my baby girl. She was the best dressed baby and she wasn't even born yet. Me and Meelah were getting by the best we could. As much as I tried to ignore my lust and attraction for men, it just wouldn't pass completely. I made love to her and was faithful to her for the most part. I had that one minor slip up with Corey in Atlanta, but as usual, he disappeared like a thief in the night after we hooked up.

He had promised me the world and whispered lots of sweet nothings in my ear. Sadly, in the end I was left with a gaping leaky ass and he was nowhere to be found. I was furious with myself for allowing him to come in and stir up those emotions inside of me, yet again. Meelah was very insecure and accused me of cheating a lot, although I wasn't...aside from that one isolated incident. My career and growing popularity were also wearing on her. While I'll admit that I wasn't fully happy with her, she was having my baby and I had to deal with the cards I'd been dealt.

Meelah had already made it quite clear that I was not welcome to be a part of our daughter's life if she and I split. The pregnancy had really changed her for the worst. I saw characteristics in her that I had never seen before. In hindsight, the warning signs had been there all along. I spent most of my free time showering her with gifts and attention. I didn't want her stressing about a thing.

Our current dilemma, as it usually was, revolved around sex or lack thereof. I did my best to immerse her in four play, but I could never stay hard enough to penetrate her. I was riddled with guilt because the one thing that brought me so much joy, was also the main thing that turned me off about her. I couldn't have sex with her with my child inside of her. How could I lie on top of her large rounded belly and have sex with her knowing our baby girl was lying in between us.

To some, I may have been a little extra, but to me it was bothersome enough to halt our sex life for a while. Don't get me wrong, Meelah glowed lighter than a 120 voltage light. I adored her from her extra wide beak, all the way down to her fat sausage toes. I just wished she could see how beautiful she was from my eyes. I was putting my all into making us a family and wasn't thinking about another chick or dude.

I just prayed she'd come to her senses before our baby came. I didn't know how much more I could take.

« Chapter 29 Blast From The Past »

"WELCOME HOME BABY brother!!!" Me and Aimee yelled as Jonah walked out of the prison that had housed him since his transfer. He was looking much better, healthier and straighter than he did at the last institution. We had threatened to sue the hell out of the prison for allowing their inmates to be violently raped on their watch.

It was nice to have the clan back together and getting along more than we ever had. We decided to celebrate his release by throwing a huge block party. Everyone that was someone would be in attendance. Since my dad was still recovering from his amputation, I had moved him, Aimee, Sky and Meelah into the mini mansion that I had purchased from the advance I'd received from a movie deal that I'd just accepted.

On the way from the prison, Aimee whispered, "I hate the way she treats you," referring to Meelah.

"Well, you understand how those raging pregnancy hormones are. Once she delivers Melanie, she will hopefully simmer down a little bit."

"I'm just saying, if the shit doesn't stop soon, I'm beating her ass just as soon as she delivers my niece!" She promised.

"Fair enough, sis. Fair enough."

"Oh and I kind of sort of invited a special guest."

Rolling my eyes I skeptically asked, "Who?"

"You'll see."

"Can I get just a little hint?" I begged with my best puppy dog face.

"Nope! You're just going to have to be patient and wait for once, superstar!"

I smacked my lips and folded my arms across my flat chest in frustration. I hated surprises.

Pulling up to my house, I could see that the band and caterers were already busy at work setting up their areas. It was already looking amazing. The caterers were serving all of our favorite southern dishes, while pops insisted on manning the grill from his wheelchair. He always wanted to contribute and do his part even with his new disability.

I gave Jonah a tour of the place and showed him where his room was. He was in total awe of how we were living. My dad's house was paid for by mama's life insurance policy, however, we all opted not to sell. Mama...hell we all loved that house. It held so much history. So many memories. There were some fantastic meals made with love in our kitchen.

I had invited some of the models and aspiring actresses that I had met along my journey and I couldn't wait for their arrival. We had security just in case anything jumped off as well. Having security at Aimee's baby shower could have potentially saved several lives. Quite a few people were coming from my old hood, so I definitely didn't want any problems.

While my dad fired up the grill and we waited for everyone to arrive, I decided to hop in the shower and get fly for the party. I knew that my dad and brother still weren't completely comfortable with my lifestyle, so I would tone it down just a bit. I couldn't guarantee that all of my guests would do the same. Since it was technically Jonah's party, we had already taken the liberty of inviting his friends from around our old neighborhood and he was free to invite those we'd overlooked.

I'd even extended an invitation to AJ, however, he and his new boo were in Vegas for the week. I was happy for him, but I sometimes wallowed in the 'what ifs'. Deep down, I knew I'd made the best decision. He was a great guy and I'd hurt him deeply. He deserved much better than I could give at that time. I often wondered if Meelah and her psychotic mood swings were my karma for having cheated and impregnating her while me and AJ were together.

I loved a lot of old school 90's and early 2000 music, however, the DJ catered to everyone's taste...even to my white friends. It felt great to be around old friends as well as the new ones. Speaking of which, Harmony and her boo Trevante were able to make it. She looked so happy. Everyone was so genuinely happy with my success and impressed with my new lifestyle. The hallways of my home were self-centeredly sprinkled with the spreads that I was most proud of.

Of course Meelah and the rest of my family had a strong photography presence too. Over the main fireplace in my downstairs family room was a huge portrait of mama looking every bit of the queen she was. I couldn't help but to stare at it every time I entered the room. It made me feel protected. As I mingled throughout the growing crowd, I couldn't help but to fill with pride as I watched my little niece and Shateara bounce on the trampoline in the backyard next to my pool.

Shateara?! If she was here, then that meant that *he* was here too!

"I'm gonna kill that heifer!" I growled.

This must've been Aimee's big surprise. She is the only person who could've or would've invited that fool. Of course, I didn't mind if my God baby was here. It was long overdue. I didn't see her nowhere near as often as I used to. But her big headed daddy had no business being anywhere near me...let alone in my house. I scanned the

Premises, but he was not in sight.

I sighed in relief. Maybe Shateara and Shateara alone was my big surprise. Surely, she was more than enough to make my heart smile. I decided to walk over to my pops throwing down at the grill to see if he could hook me up with a burger or a hot dog or something. I realized that we were so amped up about Jonah getting out today, that we had completely forgotten to eat. Well now my stomach was roaring and I needed to eat like yesterday!

"Hey pops! Can your favorite child get a little something to hold him over? A burger, pork steak or something?!" I begged like Pookie, the crackhead.

He smiled his bright smile and replied, "Only if your favorite pops can get that pan of ribs off the kitchen island in the house." He bargained.

"Deal!" I yelled taking off like a child to retrieve the pan of meat to be cooked.

I stepped into a side door that put me closest to the kitchen and saw several pans of uncooked meat ready to be grilled. I stepped closer to inspect each one until I located the ribs. My pops had his work cut out for himself. There was a lot of food and a lot of hungry people, but I was confident that he'd pull it off. If for whatever reason he couldn't, he had a lot of reinforcement ready to lift the burden.

A strange feeling took over me and the hairs on the back of my neck stood straight up. I could smell him before I could feel his presence. My stomach did summersaults, and my knees buckled as I closed my eyes praying for the good Lord to give me the strength to resist him once and for all. I was sick of our hit it and quit it song and dance. I internally patted myself on the back when I willed my budding erection to remain flaccid.

Just then, I felt his warm breath graze the back of my neck. Why was I so weak for that man? As the front of his body pressed into the rear of mine, I lost control of all of my senses for a moment. I spun around to face him and immediately regretted my decision to do so. He was looking and smelling better than sex. I pushed away because I felt it was the noble thing to do, but he was not with the shit. His body barely moved from my weak attempt to escape him.

He lifted me up onto the same island that held all the meat and stepped in between my thighs. Without uttering a word, he roughly pressed his lips upon mine and stuck his tongue down my throat. I accepted him as I always did. I was intoxicated merely by his presence. I don't know why I even bothered resisting him, in the end I always caved. I was shocked by his forwardness in such an open space. He was always so concerned about people knowing that he was into men that public displays of affection were off the table.

As his pelvis grinded into mine, I moaned like a wounded animal. Perhaps I was. I was so hurt and conflicted with the feelings I had for this man.

Just as I had leaned down to suckle on his nipple, I heard a familiar voice say, "Hey baby, pops sent me in here to see what the holdup was with the ribs?"

Panic rippled through my body as I realized that it was too late to mask the compromising position the two of us were in. No matter how I tried to spin this, the fact remained that Meelah had just caught me getting freaky with another man. It was beyond disrespectful of me and I was instantly filled with remorse. I knew better, however, in the presence of Corey my brain always ceased to function properly.

The expression covering her face and the bewildered look in her eyes told me that shit was about to get ugly. Really ugly.

"Oh my god! I fucking knew it! I knew you were cheating on me! Your ass hasn't fucked me or wanted to be bothered in God only knows how long, yet here you are with this booty buster ready to pounce! I'm so sick of this shit Junior! What do I have to do Junior? Grow a dick and a hairy set of balls for you to want me? I can't compete with that nigga. The look you have in your eyes when he's around speaks volumes. You've never looked at me like that! I fucking hate you for this Junior!!! I fucking hate you!" She screamed at the top of her lungs while lunging for me.

I stood there and allowed her to use me as a punching and scratching bag because I felt I deserved it. Hell, I was so numb that I didn't even feel the blows after the first few landed. I guess Corey knew what I was doing, however, he grew tired of witnessing the attack and removed an angry Meelah from next to me. I guess she wasn't done with me yet, because she was soon charging back over to me when all of a sudden, she doubled over in pain.

"Oh shit, baby! Are you okay? Is the baby okay?" I asked in a concerned tone.

"Get your nasty faggot hands off of me! Don't you ever touch me again. Why are you asking about *my* child? You will never see her after she is born. Get away from me!" She growled before doubling over again.

I understood that she was emotionally hurt, so I wasn't about to argue about the fucked-up shit that she was saying. What I did know was that something was happening, and she was in a lot of pain. She needed to get to the hospital immediately to see about my daughter.

"Hey Corey, stay with her while I let pops and Aimee know that I need to take her to the hospital." I ordered running back out of the same patio.

Running up to my dad, he had a displeased look on his face. I already knew he was about to bitch about me not bringing him the ribs, but fuck those ribs!

As I opened my mouth to give him a quick recap, loud shouting was taking place next to the pool. I rolled my eyes and blew an exasperated breath as I realized that it had to be one of Jonah's ghetto ass friends bringing his hood behaviors with him. I knew inviting their asses had the potential to backfire and here we were. Holding up my index finger to my dad letting him know I needed a minute, I walked over to the crowd.

Where the fuck was my security at? As I broke through the crowd, my question was answered. Both of my big burly security officers had been bound, gagged and tied. Not even thinking, I immediately stepped forward ready to untie them, when I was cracked in the back of my head with something cool and metal. Dazed I stammered backwards. It took me a few moments to refocus.

When I finally looked at my offender, I nearly shit my pants.

"Vasti, what the fuck man?! Why are you here? What are you doing, man?!"

"Nigga, shut your little dick sucking ass up! I heard you were having a little party, but you must've forgotten to send my invitation. So, I took the liberty of inviting myself." He spoke scooping up a handful of my five-tiered cake and shoving it in his mouth.

"Damn, this cake is hella moist nigga." He belted teasingly.

I was seeing red because that cake was extremely expensive and he had just ruined it with his monkey paws. He was even uglier than I remembered. I still can't believe Nami fucked him! And had a baby too!

"Awww...what's the matter little Junior? Are you gonna cry?" He taunted.

"You do know that if you do, I have just the right pacifier to shut you the fuck up." He grabbed at his crotch.

I gagged at the possibility.

"I must say. You have made quite the come up lil nigga. Who would've thought?" He asked no one in particular waving what I now knew was a gun in the air.

I originally came here to eat and to rob the place, but seeing you again reminded me of what you did and nigga you are about to die!"

"Leave my fucking brother alone!" Aimee sounded off from the crowd.

"Fuck you, bitch. That's no way to talk to the man who may be your baby's daddy. Aye Junior, did you know that we use to run trains on your sister before she became all high and mighty? We used to wear her ass out! Five, sometimes ten niggas at a time. No talent supersedes that of a crackhead in search of their next fix."

I saw Aimee's head drop from embarrassment. I felt for my sister because no matter what, she was always being reminded of her past. It was thrown in her face all the time.

I signaled to my sister to pick her head back up and she did.

I said a silent prayer that someone had alerted the police. This bum was a lunatic seeking to even the score for some shit that went down in high school.

I had to get back to Meelah and get her to the hospital.

"Look Vasti, I apologize for all the shit that took place between us in high school. Can we call a truce and let bygones be bygones?" I asked getting close enough to shake with him.

Huge mistake. Instead of shaking my hand, he shot me in it. I screamed at the top of my lungs as pain ripped through my hand. Aimee flew to my side to control the bleeding. The partygoers were paralyzed with fear and were as motionless as ice sculptures. The only person that I noticed was on the move was my pops in his electric scooter. He signaled for us all to be quiet as he slowly crept up on Vasti from behind. As he got closer, he accelerated the chair to its fastest setting and crashed into him.

Vasti fell face forward onto the ground from the impact. My dad then leaped from the chair and landed on top of Vasti trying to wrestle the gun from him. As a group of us went in to subdue Vasti, we heard a deafening, POW!

No one moved for a moment, but then we all quickly assessed ourselves for a bullet hole when Meelah dropped to the ground with a thud. It was obvious that she was dead. She had a large hole in the center of her forehead and her eyes were wide open in shock. I heard lots of people running and screaming, yet I remained motionless.

Silent tears streamed down my face as I mourned the loss of Meelah and the baby girl I'd never met. How could this happen?

I was so deep in my sadness that I barely heard Vasti scream, "No!!! Not my sister!!! You made me kill my fucking sister!!!" He raged.

Snapping out of my daze, I finally realized that he was referring to Meelah as his sister. What the fuck was really going on?

I didn't even have time to react as Vasti aimed his gun at Aimee and sent two bullets straight through her giant heart. Without batting an eyelash, he then aimed the gun at me, but as I heard another loud POP echoing through the air, I felt myself being pushed to the ground and I felt my ribs break from the shear force and weight of another body landing on top of me.

« Chapter 30 From Darkness To Light »

IT HAD BEEN TWO YEARS since the tragic blood bath in the backyard that fateful day. Who would've thought that a day that started out as a celebration would end in so much devastation? Meelah and Aimee were buried right next to Marlon and mama. I left before either of my two loves were lowered into the ground. Explaining Aimee's death to Skyy was by far one of the most difficult things I ever had to do.

She was still too young to understand death in the way that an adult would, however, I was able to get her to understand the permanency of what it meant to die. Seeing Sky shake a seemingly sleeping Aimee and begging her to wake up had me bawling like a newborn baby. There wasn't a dry eye in the church.

I was hospitalized for just under a month shortly after the funerals. I went back into sickle cell crisis brought on by the stress. I wanted to die for a long time. I was the intended target. The bullets were meant for me. The guilt had nearly taken me out.

They often say that God doesn't put more on you than what one could handle, but at the time I was full of doubt. How much death could one family take? Just as we were picking up the pieces and starting a new life together, tragedy decided to rear its ugly head yet again. I never knew that Meelah was Vasti's sister. I had lived with her and her mama briefly after I left Jean, but I had never seen Vasti or her other brothers ever. I knew that she had brothers and according to her, they were bad news and weren't welcome to the house.

How could someone so beautiful be related to such a monster?! Figuratively and literally speaking. Due to the extensive damage caused by the bullet to her forehead, my dear Meelah was forced to have a closed casket. I had come to realize that two arrests had been made after waking up in the hospital later that day. I was devastated to learn that Jonah and Vasti were the masterminds behind it all.

That boy wasn't even out a full twenty-four hours and was already back in prison. This time for good. Unbeknownst to me, Vasti had offered to pay Jonah ten grand for his participation. Jonah was the one who had subdued the security guards. They didn't expect Jonah to be up to anything shady...boy were we all wrong. Knowing that he'd ruined our family over a measly ten thousand dollars boiled my blood. I would've gladly given him that, and so much more.

Of course, as we all know, the plan didn't go as they had planned it. I was supposed to be the only one to end up in a body bag...not the ladies. And my baby girl? Well Melanie Aimee-Rose Hilton was now an inquisitive, energetic two-year-old. She was the spitting image of her mother. Perhaps the only things she'd inherited from me were my golden eyes and personality. She was such a beautiful baby.

I know you're wondering how in the hell did she survive after her host died correct? The answer is simple. With all the commotion going on around us, my pops used his military and limited medical knowledge to cut my daughter from her dead mother. He knew time was against us, but he later told me that he refused to allow his second grandchild to die if there was even a slim chance of him being able to save her. She was such a paw paw's baby. He spoiled that girl rotten.

I'd also realized that it was Corey who had shielded me from those bullets. Luckily, in his line of work, he always wore a bullet proof vest, so his injuries were minor. Apparently, Vasti had tried to take his own miserable life, but was out of bullets. Unfortunately for him, the cops didn't know that little fact when they finally showed their asses up. He kept waving that empty gun around when they arrived, so they gladly lodged a bullet into his upper back severing that portion of his spine. He would now live out the rest of his days as a quadriplegic.

That was far better karma than death in my opinion. Knowing that he'd be shitting, pissing and drooling on himself brought me great satisfaction. I hoped his ass developed bed sores down to his damn bones. Our lawyers wanted to pursue the death penalty for him and Jonah, but life in prison was justice enough. Plus, I don't think that my pops could bear to lose another child...even if he did deserve it. Jonah was eventually placed back in the same prison where he was being raped. He would now spend the rest of his days being beaten and raped.

Let's just say, my celebrity status gave me a lot of reach now. Junior would be someone's bitch every day for the rest of his miserable life. My dad cut him off too. He initially had a difficult time believing that his own flesh and blood would help orchestrate such a heinous crime. We both attended lots and lots of therapy to come remotely close to some sense of normalcy. While I thought about Mama, Aimee, Marlon and Meelah every day, I could finally make it through my days without crumbling now.

I sold that house because I could never find the courage to step foot back in there. I ended up purchasing an even bigger and better one a few streets away. I loved the area and the school district was perfect for Skyy, Melanie and Shateara. Yes Shateara, too. Nu Nu had completely surrendered her parental rights to Shateara and I legally adopted Shateara and Skyy. Naturally, I stepped up to the plate after Aimee was murdered and took over custody of my niece.

I thought back to the conversation she and I had about me taking Skyy should something happen to her. I guess her destiny here on Earth was finally fulfilled. God called my sweet sister home. While I didn't like it, I had to trust his will. Speaking of sisters, I had finally met Corey's sister Adryenne. She was super sweet and so intelligent. She had just passed the bar exam. Adryenne was officially an attorney now. Corey couldn't have been prouder.

I suppose experiencing a near death experience put a lot of things into perspective for Corey. It made him realize that all of the things he feared, such as what people thought about him and I being together no longer mattered anymore. I'd be lying if I said the shit happened overnight, because it didn't. I made his ass attend some of my therapy sessions too. He eventually started to grow more and more comfortable with revealing his true self.

After the tragedies and my hospital stay, I took a six-month hiatus just to focus on the family and loved ones that I had left. Corey was extremely supportive through it all. I made one more lifestyle change that I had previously been too afraid to do. I was now living full-time as a woman. My legal name is now Merlana. Truth be told, Corey seemed to really like the new me and I think the fact that I was more feminine helped him with his own insecurities. I couldn't help but to fall more and more in love with that man every day.

My pops had learned to get up and walk again with the use of his prosthetic leg. He has since moved back into our newly renovated family home. He had actually found someone special and I really like her for him. She wasn't mama, but she did make him happy and she looked after him. Harmony was now married with another bun in the oven. She had finished her nursing program and was now working as a Registered Nurse in the same nursing home that I had abruptly abandoned years ago.

Jacoby had been arrested for human trafficking underage kids. They buried him under the jail. I had heard that Nami was picking up the pieces that Vasti and his crime had caused. She ended up delivering a healthy baby boy. With the support of her family, she was able to complete cosmetology school. I had no ill feelings for her. I prayed that she eventually opened up her beauty salon.

As for Corey and I…we were planning our upcoming wedding. I finally felt fulfilled…somewhat. We had three gorgeous girls and booming careers. He had managed to completely clean his money up and had just opened up a third night club called Merlana's. We were finally the power couple I'd always dreamt of us being. I couldn't wait to be Mrs. Wilkerson! I was about to kick his ass though, if he didn't stop calling me a 'nigga'!!!

I still hated that damn word!!!

Stay Tuned!!!

The Whore Next Door: Welcome to Thotville

Available Now!!!

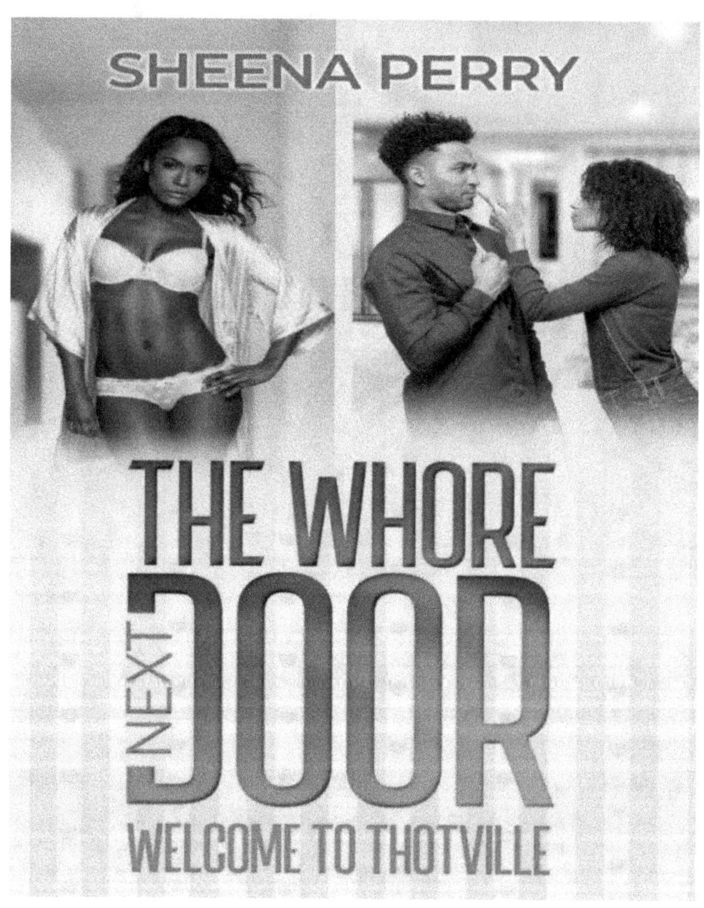

Do No Harm: License To Kill

Is Coming soon!!!

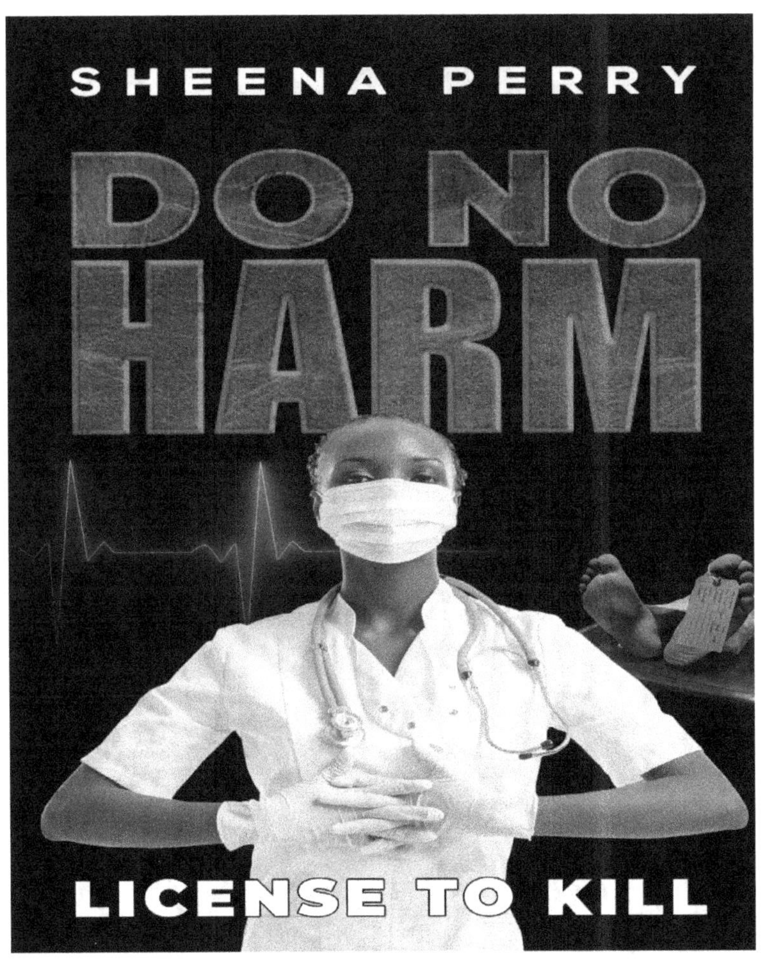

Inevitable Deceptions: A Heart's Journey To Nowhere 3

Is Coming soon!!!

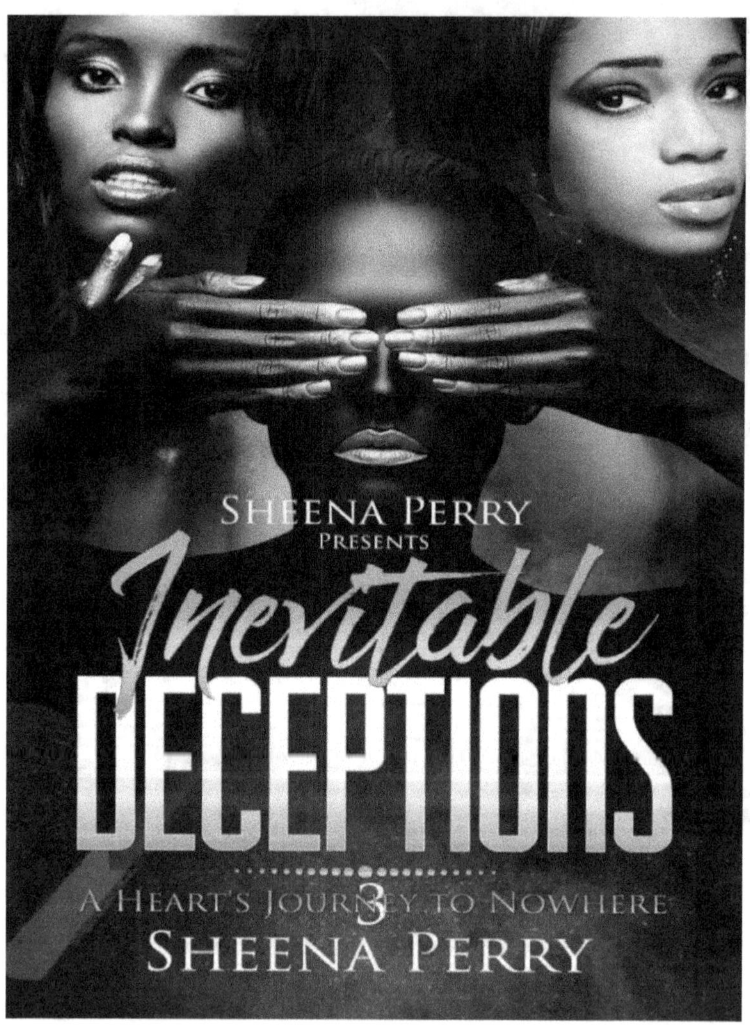

Inevitable Deceptions: A Heart's Journey to Nowhere 1

Available Now!!!

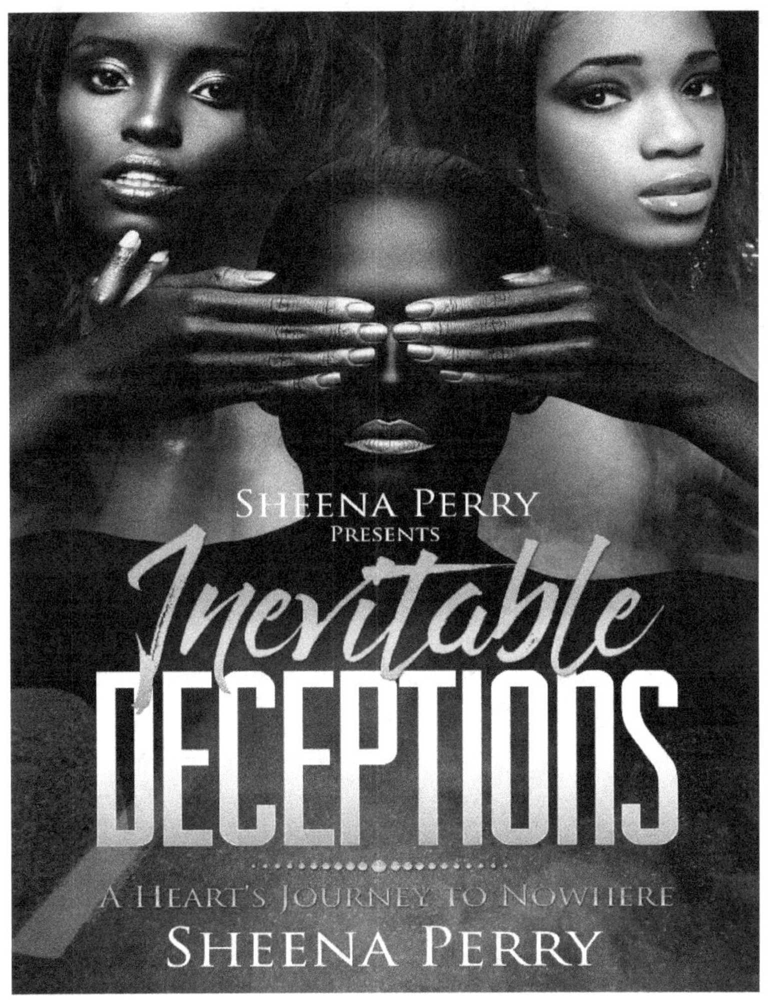

Inevitable Deceptions: A Heart's Journey to Nowhere 2

Available Now!!!

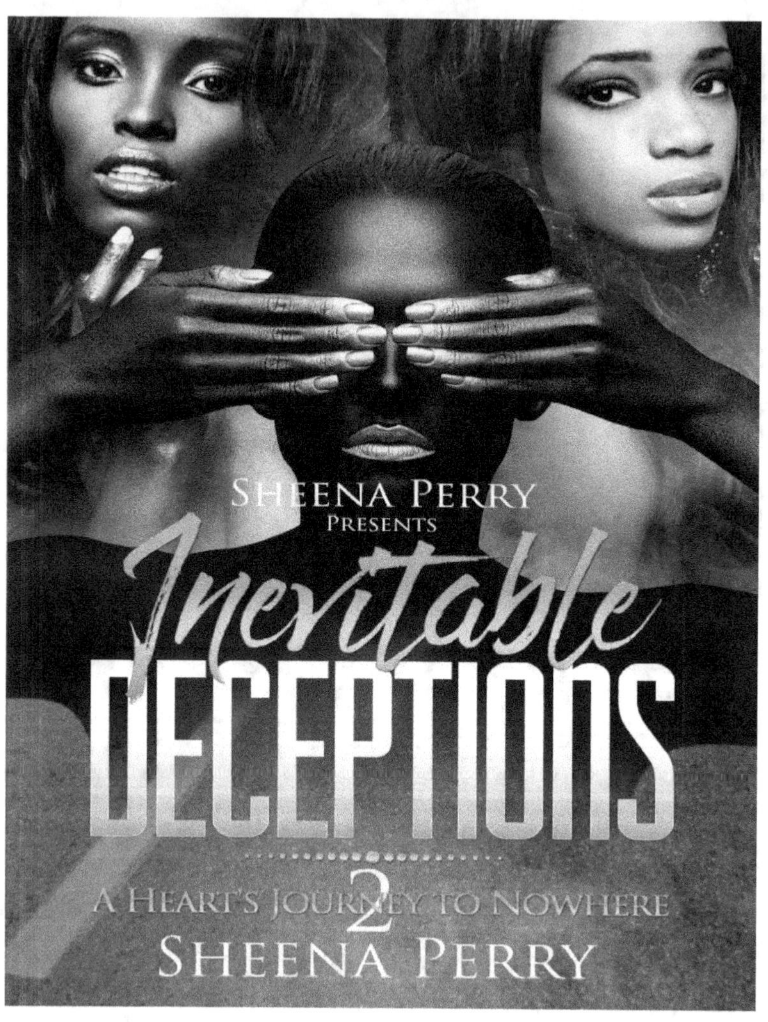

My Wife's Daughters

Available Now!!!

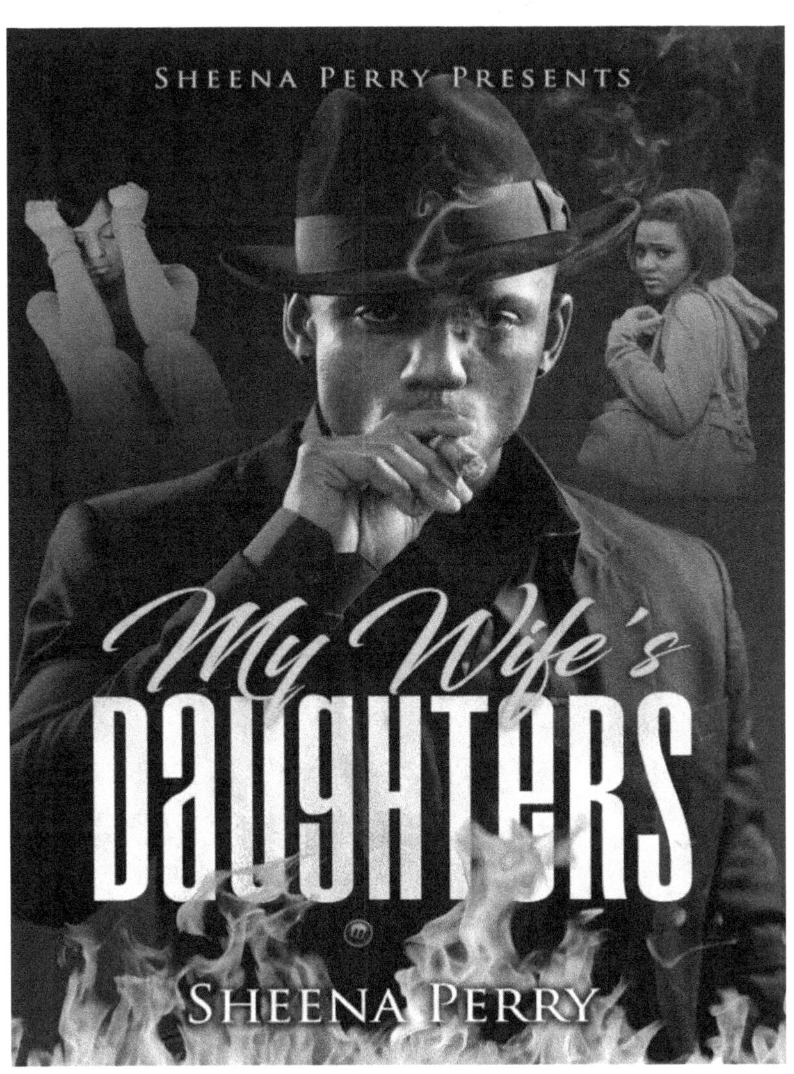

They Call Me Junior: A Gay Love Story

Available Now!!!

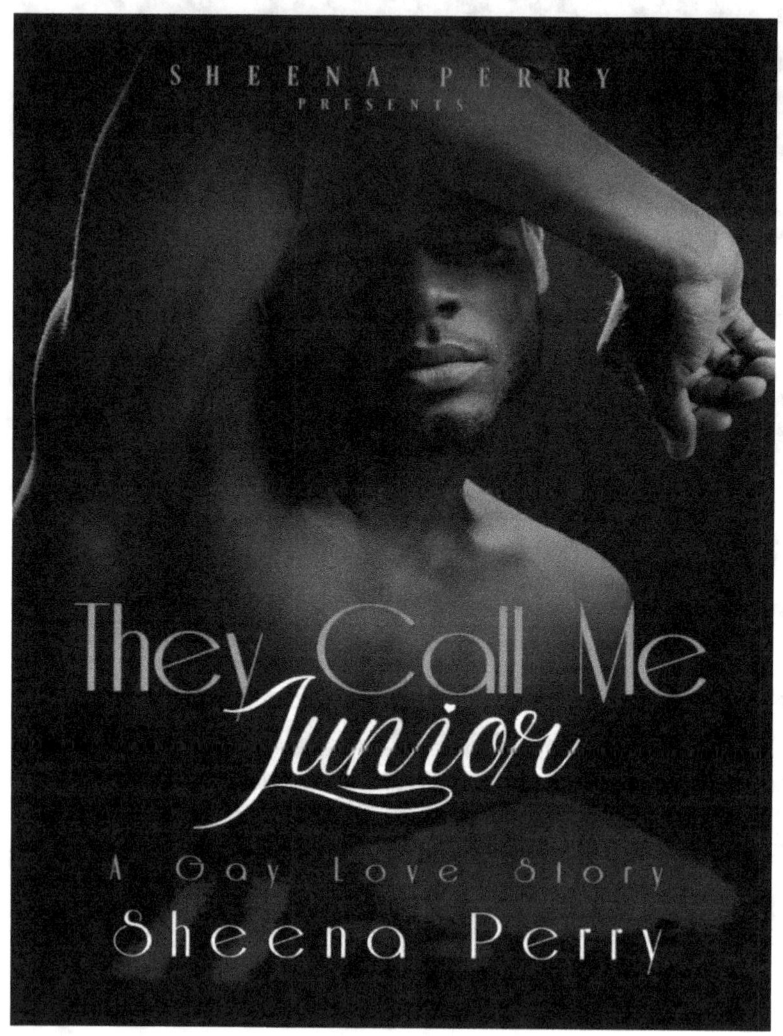

They Call Me Junior: A Gay Love Story

Available Now!!!

Releases From Other Authors

Available Now!!!

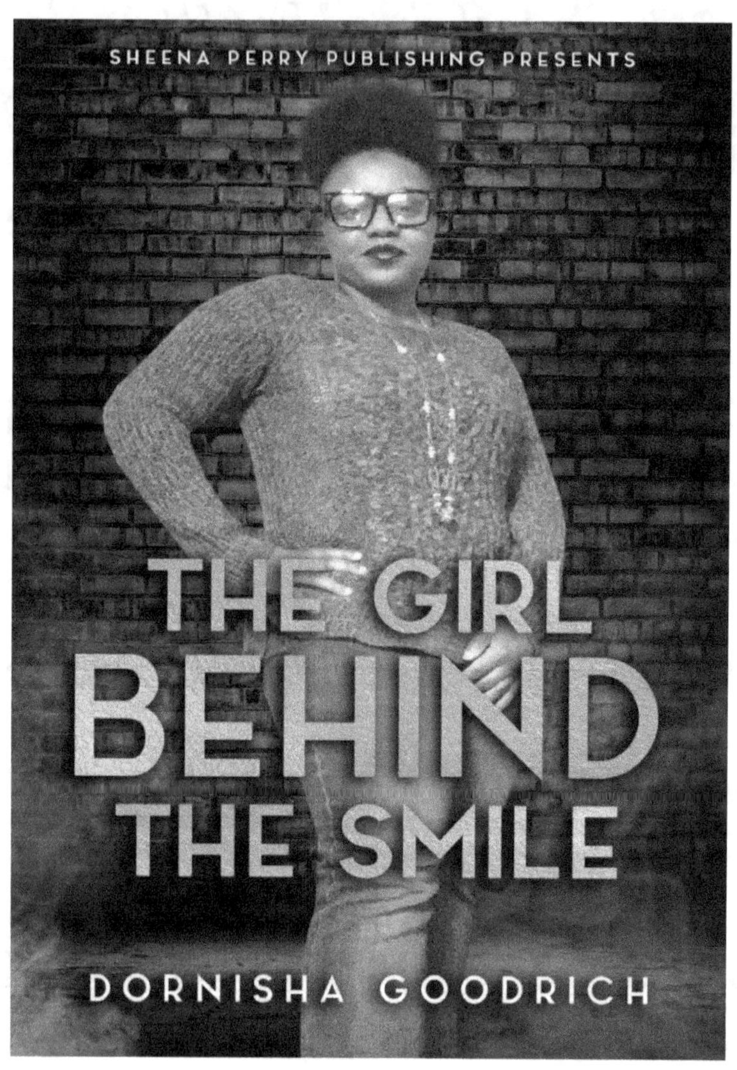

Releases From Other Authors

Available Now!!!

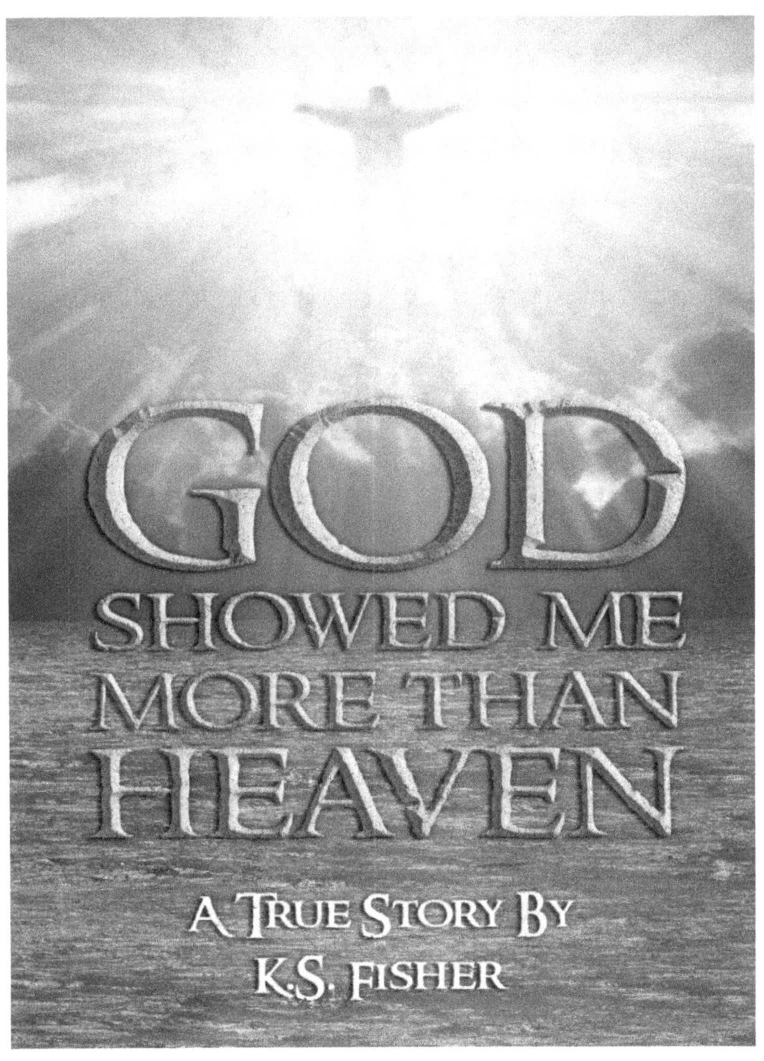

Releases From Other Authors

Available Now!!!

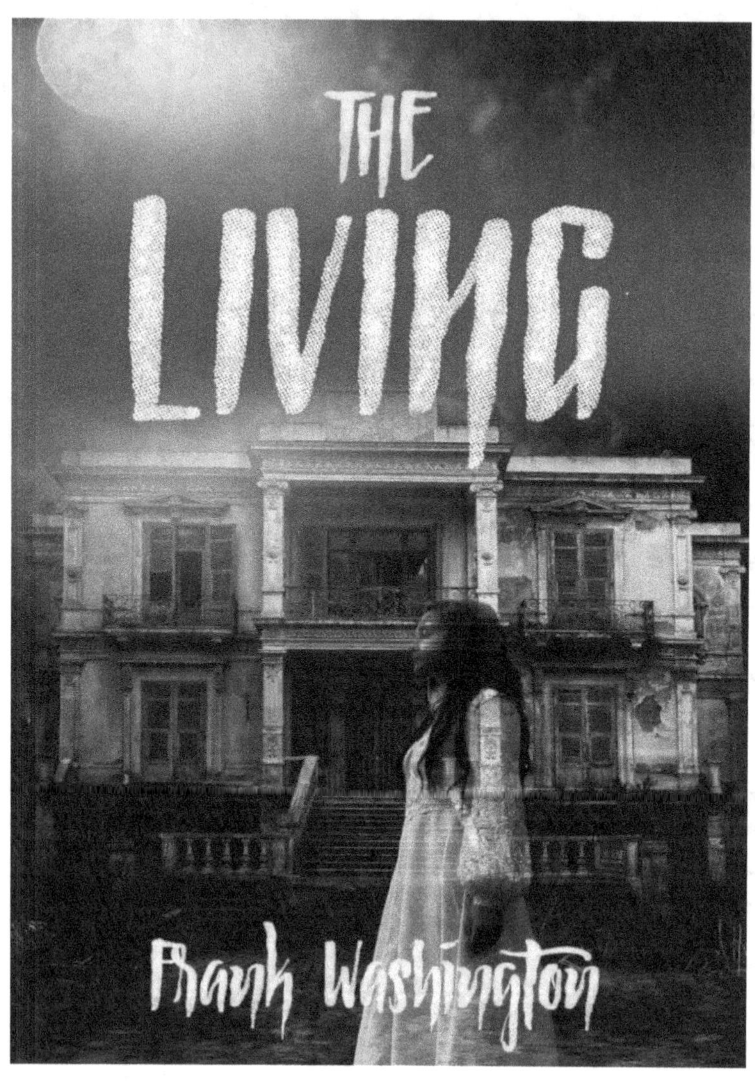

Releases From Other Authors

Is Coming soon!!!

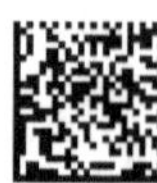
www.ingramcontent.com/pod-product-compliance
Lightning Source LLC
Chambersburg PA
CBHW070101260626
47160CB00004B/1277
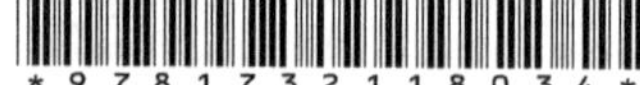
9781732118034